SECOND EDITION

QUIRKY STORIES & POEMS

Backwards, Forward & Upside Down

CHARLES BINS

5830 E 2nd St, Ste 7000 #9983
Casper, WY 82609
USA

About the Author

Charles Bins is a former journalist and marketing PR pro who has ghost-written hundreds of articles for magazines. For three decades, he executed winning campaigns for companies spanning business, technology and consumer products. Before starting his own marketing PR agency, he spent 17 years with a leading agency in New York City representing such clients as Sprint, Dow Chemical, Hewlett-Packard and Armstrong Floors.

Early in his career, he worked for the Bergen Record in N.J. and then became an internationally syndicated entertainment columnist reviewing films and interviewing celebrities including Tom Hanks, Kenny Rogers and Patty Duke. Bins earned an M.S. in Marketing/E-Commerce from the City University of New York, and a B.A. in Mass Communications from Rutgers University in N.J.

Now that he's retired, he's mostly focused on fiction. He lives with his wife, Mary, two cats and a cockatoo in Leland, N.C.

I dedicate this book to my grandchildren,
Sarah and Alanna, who might find as
much laughter, wisdom and inspiration
in these pages as I do in their lives.

Foreword

During my career as a journalist, copywriter, marketer and public relations professional, I enjoyed writing about both people and things.

As an internationally syndicated entertainment columnist, I reviewed some iconic films such as "The Fog," "Alien" and "Caddyshack." Columbia Pictures made the 1978 press opening of "Caddyshack" a splash with an outdoor party at Rockefeller Center in Manhattan. It was July, so instead of skaters, about 500 movie people jammed the lower plaza jostling elbow to elbow. They were flanked by long spreads featuring chefs slicing roast beef, and fountains gushing chocolate. With the glistening statue of Prometheus flying in front of the waterfall and passerbys ogling the crowd from above, the party lasted into the evening. Many went out afterwards.

Still, the stars arrived early for the 11 a.m. press conference the next day at Dangerfield's club on First Avenue. Director Harold Ramis, Ted Knight and Rodney Dangerfield were gathering on the stage in back on barstools while Chevy Chase tickled the keys of a baby grand and Bill Murray snatched a Bloody Mary from the bar. At 11:01 a.m., Murray waved in a pizza guy from the front door, paid him, then carried the box one-handed to a table by his barstool. He opened the box and pulled out a gooey wedge. Just as he was about to lower it into his mouth, he paused, looked around sheepishly and asked, "Anybody want a slice?"

There were only about a dozen reporters there, and at age 22, I was the youngest. So when they opened the floor to questions, I was surprised someone else didn't raise their hand first. (Maybe they all partied late.) In any case, I thought Dangerfield was the film's stand-out but had noticed Chevy Chase was listed first in the opening credits. So I hoped my question would spark some colorful interaction: "With all due respect to Mr. Chase, how did you all decide who got top billing?"

Chase pointed to the director. Ramis replied: "It was all alphabetical."

No sizzle there…Another reporter (whose caffeine had now kicked in) tried to join me in the hunt for color. The stars of the show, however, had apparently pre-agreed to mutual kindness and droned on about what great buds they were on the set. (*Boring*.) So while in my opinion Rodney Dangerfield stole the show, Bill Murray stole the press briefing.

Although I only worked in the entertainment industry for a few years, I became an internationally syndicated columnist and interviewed about one star a week, mostly from TV. Among many others this included: singer Anne Murray before her first Christmas special, Patty Duke in the TV remake of "The Miracle Worker," Kenny Rogers when he became "The Gambler," Robert Guillaume when "Benson" was running the governor's mansion, and Tom Hanks when he started making it 'big' with his first network TV show, "Bosom Buddies." I also interviewed behind-the-scenes people like jingle writers, producers (including the producers of "Three's Company") and even a stuntman who got paid for setting himself on fire.

*

During my 30 years in marketing and PR (about half spent at a leading agency in New York City), I worked with many lesser known, but also stellar, people from diverse fields including: computers and telecommunications, chemistry, food, construction and agriculture. (Farmers are among the most solid people on Earth, perhaps because they are so close to it.)

As a PR pro, I've ghost-written hundreds of business and technical articles for trade magazines. Fortunately, I enrolled in a technical writing course as an undergraduate at Rutgers (and was the only non-engineering student in the class). I also took courses in creative writing and advertising copywriting while on the National Student Exchange Program at the University of Alabama. My most important college writing class though was English grammar. --You can't fake the mechanics, and the structure of language (as Noam Chomsky details in his introductory book) is about making ideas clear.

My corporate clients over the years included several household names, even if some have since faded from view: Panasonic, Hewlett-Packard, Dow Chemical, Armstrong Floors and Sprint PCS. I was adept at explaining technical concepts and industry issues in an interesting way and always enjoyed learning new things. So I have written about diverse topics such as: waterproofing the new World Trade Center, predicting color trends in interior design, reducing foodborne pathogens in poultry processing, and the role of 3D-printing in the future of automotive manufacturing. Many topics were truly arcane. How many can say they've written about how aluminum melts, how food freezes or how paint dries?

Public relations is often about dealing with difficult issues. Every industry faces challenges, but how a company chooses to deal with an issue or challenge can speak volumes and echo far into the future. Attorneys often hold sway over management decisions in difficult situations. They generally favor saying as little as possible out of fear a statement will be used in court later. Since corporate officers can often be held accountable, this can create a chilling effect. Silence though, can be deafening when the public is demanding answers, and "no comment" is just as bad. Both erode trust and build resentment. From the PR side, dialogue is important if only to say, "We are investigating, and will keep you apprised as we go." Of course, the best strategy is to always build trust *before* something happens.

I have witnessed an array of issues, and our clients were usually the protagonists when it came to protecting human health and the environment. I am proud to have worked with corporate leaders and represented companies that fought to improve drinking water and food safety, reduce accidents and injuries, improve air quality and fuel economy, and boost the efficiency of recycling. Issues are not always black-and-white, however, and there are often trade-offs. In my opinion, two parties need to fully understand the other's point of view in order to successfully negotiate solutions. Too often, people make judgements with incomplete and often erroneous information, an alarming problem that is intensifying. This duality is the subject of my story, "Black and White."

*

I wrote this book to explore both serious and playful ideas that have percolated up, starting from a young age. The first dozen pieces are suitable for reading aloud to children. There are a few stories such as "Sister Mary Judas Roars" and "Family Spring Break, Anyone?" (as well as some poems) that are based on real events, but almost all are fiction. I included a children's story that I wrote in high school, "The Boy Who Loved Grape Jam," and a science-fiction story I wrote in college, "The Diamond Affair." However, almost all have been written over the past 15 years, which spans that gaping pothole in American history known as The Great Recession. The malaise lingered too long for me and is perhaps best captured in my poem about resentment titled, "Harbor." Many of the stories and poems include an author's note at the end to give further context.

Most of my poems were written 10 or 20 years ago. I don't claim to be a master of the form, and my style leans more to Shel Silverstein than The Bard. Still, I am drawn to it as a craftsman to a fine tool. Poetry is exquisitely useful for distilling ideas and excavating emotions. I also enjoy the sound and rhythm of poems as the playfulness of a friend.

Since my retirement, I have been writing more regularly thanks to my weekly writing group, Carolina Coastal Writers. The idea for the title of this book came from a cat-loving retired English teacher in my group who said, "Your stories tend to be a little quirky." I decided she was right. One of the quirkiest here is "Bobblehead," a satirical farce generated in one of our group's 20-minute sessions before the 2022 mid-term elections. However, if quirky also encompasses serendipity, "It Would Only

Take a Second," is the quirkiest if you consider the author's note that follows it.

For this first edition, I gravitated to pieces under 600 words, which was the maximum for the monthly *Cape Fear Voices* (www.cfvts.org) where I have been a layout editor and a regular contributor. It's a good cause: The non-profit supports young writers.

When I first started writing for the publication, it was only printed in black-and-white, and I thought I would try my hand at cartooning to liven it up. I produced my first cartoon for the Halloween story "Red Wagon" after a cartoonist on You-Tube said, "If you think you can't draw faces, start by drawing two sixes for the eyes." I was hooked and have often spent more time on the cartoon than the story. (All the drawings are mine.)

This book may not win any awards, but I had great fun writing these pieces and I hope you enjoy at least some of them, too.

Charles "Chuck" Bins

PS:
Stay tuned. I am continuing to write short stories and will soon compile them in a second book. Most are in the 1,500 to 2,000-word range and they include stories that are quirky, poignant and often both. Learn more, and keep in touch on my author website: charlesbins.com

Quirky Stories & Poems
Backwards, Forward & Upside Down

Table of Contents

Backwards: Real and imagined stories looking back

Part 1 (for kids and kids at heart)

Part 2 (for teens and adults)

Forward: Stories gazing into the future

Upside Down: Stories from the edge

Backwards:

Real and imagined stories looking back...
To younger years and days gone by,
To early fears and joys,
To a time of wonder.

To school days,
From kindergarten to middle school and high
From schoolyard dares and hormones
To real love and crushed hearts.

There's scary stories, too,
A family vacation,
poems to ponder, and more.

Just turn the page and see...

This poem was inspired in part by a ditty that my father weaned us on:
*Johnny, Johnny strong and able, suddenly died at the breakfast
table Said his little sister Meg, "Can I have his other egg?"*

Breakfast with Johnny (and Meg)

It all started at the breakfast table
Feeding us from those silly little jars
With that disgustingly cute baby on the label.

Little Johnny gets stringy a-spar-a-gus.
Meg smiles like the baby Gerber
Or is she making fun of Johnny?

"Green -- good for you," mouths Meg.
"Goo-goo-goo good," Mom begs,
More wincing than convincing.
(They're ganging up good.)
"Goo-goo" is all Johnny can say
But today he just wants an egg.

You know you could, the fridge is right there.
So what if he's in diapers and not underwear
Like big girl, Meg, bubbling her bananas
(Tomorrow she gets to go to Nanas.)
Johnny folds arms -- and not just for show.
Today he learns a fresh word: "No!"

At that, Mom stops feeding Meg
Turns off her coddling charms
Turns on the Ice Queen stare
"Drat, don't you dare!"

Raspberry lips curl to a frown
Drizzling stringy asparagus down

The baby bib and onto the berber

Mom gets up, racing for the towels
Johnny gets *déjà vu* down in his bowels
A new lesson (ya think?)
Not yet: "No!

"You rascal," says Mom aglow
-- Not in a good way though
Cleaning up the mess and Johnny.

Meg's laughing now, "Tee-hee-hee, hee-hee!"
Johnny can't stomach it; greens not on his diet.
"No!" he wails. "I want my Meg" (?) "Mmy-yeg!"
Mom turns slowly with a wink of an eye:
"I see," says she, "You just want an egg."

Author's Note:
A chemical engineer, my father wrote poetry in college and would often impress us by reciting Shakespeare and famous poems from memory. (Our family favorite -- "The Cremation of Sam McGee" – is a sonnet by the lesser-known Robert W. Service and is truly a howl.)

When I attended Rutgers University in in the early '70s, all freshmen were required to take English composition. In my first class, we spent 20 minutes writing about something we hated, then we exchanged stories, and a classmate could read one aloud if they liked it. Mine, titled "I Hate Spinach," captured the point of view of a baby strapped in a highchair with his mother trying to feed him "from that bottle with the disgustingly cute baby on the label." The class loved it, and I spent my career writing, first as a journalist and syndicated entertainment columnist and then as a marketing PR pro and senior advertising copywriter.

The Boy Who Loved Grape Jam

Being seven years old, not too many things made sense to me. But grape jam did, and I loved it. In fact, the only thing that made sense to me was grape jam and, of course, George, my teddy bear.

As I crawled into my bed, the sheets were just as I liked them -- cool and snug. The grape-colored walls of my room were now dark. Grotesque shadows danced on the walls like giant spiders. Glancing over at my closet, I sensed someone's presence. I knew it was the wicked old man who hid in my closet every night. I prayed that he would not jump out and kidnap me and George tonight.

I held onto George tightly and tried to think of peaceful things, but the only thing I could think of was grape jam. Then I remembered the jar under my bed. Quietly, so as not to disturb the old man in the closet, I wrapped my hand around the jar and tried to pick it up, but it stuck to the rug a little. The lid made an eerie sound as I unscrewed it. I set the top on the pillow next to George and sunk my fingers into the sweet ooze. The jam tasted a little old, but it tasted better after I scraped the mold off the surface. Instinctively, I held George in one hand and ate the jam with the other.

I awoke in the midst of a green and bustling forest. Next to me was an open jar of grape jam which I immediately began eating. I started walking through the forest slurping the jam as I went. The sweet sensations relaxed me. The leaves and twigs crackled under my feet.

Suddenly, almost from nowhere, an eight-foot bear appeared. Live bears never made much sense to me, especially eight-foot black bears. Scared out of my pajamas, I ran hugging the jar under my arm. The bear chased after me. He was swift and I was rather slow.

"I must get away! What did this hairy beast want from me?" I thought. –"It must be my jam. At that moment, I decided: I will keep the jam. I must have it. My decision made a lot of sense to me.

The bear was faster than I, so I had to find protection fast. I looked around observing everything as I ran, but I saw only trees and, of course, an eight-foot bear! "Trees—yes, that's it! I'll climb a tree. This must be the most logical decision I've ever made," I thought proudly.

I shimmied up the tallest tree available as fast as I could, still holding the precious jar of jam. When I climbed what I judged was well out of the bear's reach, I stopped and stuffed my face with the sweet goo, which calmed me down.

The bear caught up and stopped at the bottom, watching me in despair. The gawky-looking beast attempted to shake me out of my nest, but the tree stood firm. I laughed. What a stupid animal. I slurped the jam and thought how smart I was to think of climbing a tree.

When the bear started climbing the tree, I stopped laughing. Bears that climbed trees didn't make sense to me. So I climbed higher, devouring the jam as I went. "You can have it when I'm through. It's mine," I screamed back. But the deaf bear would not listen.

I held the jar tightly as I pushed my head through the top of the prickly pine. I was almost in the bear's clutches. With my two fingers, I struggled to finish the last ounce of jam clinging to the sides of the jar. Then the bear swung his powerful arm, and I watched my precious jar fall to the ground. I cursed at the dumb bear and then leapt out of the tall tree after it. Now this made sense to me, I thought as I plummeted earthward, a lot of sense.

The bright sun glared through my purple curtains and lit my grape-colored walls. My bedroom seemed especially grapey that morning. Why I could almost smell the grapes.

An empty jar of grape jam was tucked under my arm and George's head was in the bottle. At first, I thought George had eaten all the jam, but I knew he couldn't have – the sticky goo was all over my pajamas. I tried to get out of bed, but I was stuck.

Author's Note:
I wrote this for my high school's creative magazine as a sophomore in 1971 under the title, "I Love Grape Jam If It's Not Too Sticky." I later became editor-in-chief of the school newspaper, *The Phenix*. (Thank you, Mr. Rogers!)

Stuck on You

Certainly, you know that special glue called "super"?
Well, hold your horses there's even super-duper.

The girl with the dimple said it would be simple
If only on this bright sunny day I'd say, "I do."
Didn't she know, I only agreed to more iced tea?
Yet she ardently wanted to marry me
And ride on a horse into the sunset.

"Of course," I replied, "but not quite yet…
Let me sit for a while and think on this."
She said, "You know, we'll always live in bliss."
I thought a minute, and this is what I thunk:
"Always" is a word with a fragrance of skunk.

Now I just want to skedaddle and skidoo,
But then there's the saddle and the glue.

Author's Note:
I wrote this around 2012 thinking back on the dating scene about no one in particular.

Unclog Your Thinking

Where does water go
When it goes down the drain?
I scratch my head, and strain my brain:
To Timbuktu and back again
Or only halfway to Michigan?

It could travel the clouds for hours
To water exotic Rain Forest flowers.
Or it could go to the end of a hose
To put out a fire atop high towers.

It could help grow organic clothes,
--a wardrobe for the Greener class--
Or help turn waste into methane gas.
Who, pray tell, who, who really knows?

Water could go almost anywhere,
If the drain's not clogged with Sis's hair!

Author's Note:

One day, when my daughters were young, my wife contacted me at the office to say that she had needed to call the plumber because the upstairs tub was clogged, and she didn't want me to be shocked to see the hole in the wall over the basement stairs when I got home.

Later, as I surveyed the damage, I was informed that it would have cost even more if the plumber also had to repair the wall under the stairs. I only wanted to know what caused the clog. "This," she said, holding up a thumb-sized plastic doll. "It was lodged in the pipe. It took him an hour and a half to get it out, and he finally had to cut the drain."

Isn't that doll one of the quintuplets?" I asked.

When the answer came back, 'yes,' my voice went shrill: "Where are the other four?"

The Boy Who Was
Afraid of the Dark

Seymour was afraid of the dark. And without his teddy bear he was even more frightened. As hard as he tried, he couldn't find his friend Mr. Teddy Bear. Still his mother insisted that he go to sleep.

But Seymour thought there was an animal in the closet.

So his mother brought him a nightlight.

Yet Seymour still thought there was an animal in the closet, and he was too frightened to move.

When he awoke, he was in a big, dark cave. He knew the cave must be very large because he could hear his echo. "Is anybody there – there – there? But only his echo answered.

At first Seymour did not know which way to go. He couldn't see anything. And Seymour was afraid of the dark.

"Which way do I go," he thought to himself. "This way?" he asked the cave.

"This way...This way...This way," his echo answered.

Seymour put his hand out in front of him and started walking toward his echo. He kept walking until he came upon the great rock walls which held him captive. He put one hand on the rock and started walking around the great room. "Is this the right way? he said out loud.

"Right way...Right way...Right way" the echo replied.

The room was not quite so large as Seymour had imagined it. Finally, he discovered an opening in the great rock which Seymour decided must be a tunnel. The boy wondered if there were bats inside. He listened, but he could only hear his heart beating pit-a-pat, pit-a-pat, pit-a pat. Seymour did not want to stay in that room, so he entered the tunnel.

The tunnel was long, winding and dark. He scraped his knees on the rocks and tore holes in his pajamas as he crawled.

Finally, he stopped to rest. In the distance, he heard a rush of water. Even though he could not see, he knew this must be the right way. Seymour went around a bend in the tunnel, and then another – and then he saw a circle of light. The circle of light got bigger and bigger as he crawled along.

At the end of the tunnel was his bedroom. He knew where everything was in his room, and he could see everything clearly. But his nightlight was not on.

Somehow, he was not afraid of the dark now. He walked over to the closet. Sitting behind his toybox in the back of his closet was his lost teddy bear. "Why were you hiding from me, Mr. Teddy Bear?" Seymour asked. He hugged his bear and went back to sleep.

"Did you sleep well, Seymour?" his mother asked the following morning.

"Oh, yes, Momma. And when I woke up, Mr. Teddy Bear was sleeping beside me."

"Oh, really?" she asked.

"Yes, Momma. And he whispered something in my ear. He told me I wouldn't be needing that nightlight anymore."

"Oh, Seymour," she said hugging him.

Seymour looked up at her. "I think he's right momma."

Author's Note:

I wrote this in 1977 and drew several illustrations (long lost) which I hope you can imagine:

The shivering boy peering out from under the covers, the great walls of the echoing cave, Seymour's circuitous route through the tunnel, a top view of his illuminated bedroom showing his toybox, and Seymour standing before his mother in the morning hugging his teddy bear.

Tribute to the Goops

Did you ever hear of the Goops –
Roguish kids who like to say "oops"
After deliberately dropping a holiday platter
To count all the pieces into which it will shatter?

It's Saturday night: Here come the Randall's
Mother's distinguished dinner guests
Time for Mother to light the candles
While Goops pick a fight and beat their chests.

Mr. Randall is father's out-of-town boss
Fill him with visions and office dross
A seasoned meal, delightful chatter
It could help Dad jump up the ladder
Mother tried to warn him before – tsk, tsk, tsk.
"Dear, you really ought to consider the risk."

Mrs. Randall comments now sipping her tea:
"What nice boys, June, they seem so sweet to me."
The twins play blocks and Legos on the hardwood floor
But it's "Eye of the Storm" before she'll head for the door.

*

Back in my childhood, Dad read *The Goops* to me
Soon after I became a toilet-trained tot
To teach what I should and aught not
Like always say "please" and "thankee"
And don't touch your nose without a hanky.

*

But Goops, you see, are a mirror of manners – *Not!*
From hands to wall goes greasy green spot.
One Goop pokes his brother in the belly and face
Now it's time to scratch, shriek -- and chase!

With a jerk comes an elbow, knocking tea platter.
Up goes the sugar, down comes pot, splash and clatter
Mrs. Randall jumps, "It's a wee hot all over me"
Sugar rains down, frosting hairdo and dress
Goops dart away as Mother surveys the mess.

Quickly, Mother grabs broom, dustpan and towel
Father banishes boys to their room with a scowl
Mom sweeps the dress with the towel loosely
Mr. Randall frowns, father pardons profusely.

Mrs. Randall is really OK, or so she does say
She really doesn't want to make a great big fuss:
"I see it was all just an accident at play.
When it's time for turkey, hope they can join us."

She says it sincerely, not upset, no jest
(Fateful words from a misguided guest.)

Grover, the dog, is sleeping, but the table is set

The turkey's now done, the pie not yet
The Goops say they're "really sorry"
But, oops, they're really, really *not*
It's not in their vocabulary, nor guilt
A feeling that would hamper their plot.

The Goops, you see, are savages and bent on revenge
Like Morlocks with daggers on solstice at Stonehenge.

Locked in our bedroom is just not right
One little accident shouldn't spoil the night
Two mishaps maybe, or maybe a few more
Will send the Randall's limping for the door.

The Goops sit quietly, two toads through dinner
Heads hanging low, looking quite the sinner.

"Children should be seen and not heard"
That's the opinion of Mr. "Big Deal" Randall
Who absently passes finger through candle.

While parents chit-chat ad *nauseum* and laugh
The Goops are plotting a museum-piece wrap
In their schizoid hearts they chant and sing
We'll make Mr. Big Deal pay for that little gaffe
Tie them all in knots with a tiny bit of string.

Of course, Goops love ice cream and blueberry pie
So they'll wait until after dessert to spring the trap
For now, one saves a turkey drumstick in his lap
But the more plates the messier, oh my, my, my
And they'll love to see Mrs. Randall turn red and cry.

They lure Grover over at dinner to keep him close by
With zucchini and cheese, bits of carrots and chick peas.

Then pulling a bit of twine from his pocket, one Goop
Carefully lassos Grover's tail with a hangman's loop,
Under hands the end to his twin, and sets down his drink
Brother knows the signal, gives a quick wink-wink.

The first Goop makes the play reaching for a third piece of pie
Knocks over Mrs. Randall's sparkling Beaujolais: *Time to die.*

Father glares at the two once accused
"Boys, you Goops! -- Please be excused."

Now it's time for the bomb...tock-tick...tock-tick.
The other gets up, says, "Let me take a drumstick."
Grover had eyes on the prize every second of the meal
Goop swings the meaty stick low for the bulldog to steal.

As the naughty boy heads for dining room door
Grover follows with a woosh-woosh, clash and roar
Tail pulling tablecloth s-l-o-w-l-y, not Harry Houdini
Down comes China plates, and what's left of the zucchini.

Mr. & Mrs. Randall make a hasty excuse and exit in a daze
Father dodges a black eye but misses the bump and a raise.

Now that I look back at the Goops some decades later
Then down at my two gurgling boys (who are twin)
I suddenly wonder what kind of trouble I'm in.

Hey, Dad, wanna see what we can do?
In their highchairs, they don't stop to chew
On cue, they spew corned beef and po-taters
Cheeks to shins, grinning like crazy alligators.

Author's Note:
I wrote this poem in the style of Gelett Burgess, author of *GOOPS and How to Be Them*, a Manual of Manners for Polite Children, originally published in 1900. Burgess also illustrated the book whose simple black-and-white drawings are as hilarious as the poems. If you are not familiar with the brood consider: *"The Goops they lick their fingers, /And the Goops they lick their knives, /They spill their broth on the tablecloth -/Oh, they lead disgusting lives.*

My father (b. 1928) read The Goops to us, not just because he wanted his five children of the '50s to behave, but because my grandmother (b. 1903) had read it to her two boys. Very likely my great-grandmother had also read it to her children.

Night Noises

Bradley always loved his grandfather's visits. Before bedtime, he'd fill Bradley with stories of WWII pilots flying Tigers, of hunters on Safari tracking Big Game, and Egyptian Kings building Empires rising from the desert.

Tonight Bradley hears a strange noise, and an owl outside keeps asking, "Who, who?" He rules out house creaks and moans from the radiator. He thinks the answer might be under his bed. *Something's breathing.*

He hugs his knees and shivers. Soon his grandfather's words drift into his head: "One must always move in the face of fear." Bradley grits his teeth and prays for a sip of courage. With a deep breath, he leaps from bed and hops backward so the thing can't grab his ankles. Yet when he peers under the bed, nothing.

Bradley freezes, listening. He zeroes in on the closet. In a flash, he grabs his lightsaber and jerks the door open. Sitting there is a boy wrapped in tatters, a mummy. Seeing Bradley, the mummy lunges. The two wrestle until they nearly turn to butter. Finally, Bradley gets a knee up and pins him. "What are you doing here?"

If the mummy is rattled, he doesn't show it. "Just looking for fun. --Got any games?"

"Plenty. How 'bout you?"

"Not really," says the mummy, "but I can take you for a ride if you want."

The mummy reaches over his shoulder and unfurls a long mat painted with flat people, standing sideways in a line bearing gifts. From the clothes Bradley figures Egyptian mothers must spend all day ironing. He studies the strange letters. "What's it say?"

The mummy seems to smile. "Open the window, hold on, and I'll show you."

Slowly, they circle above the trees and sail through dark clouds. They can see stars twinkling and the earth below, spinning fast. Halfway around, the mummy finally says, "I'm from down there."

They swoop low and fly across a desert, passing trains of camels with Bedouins trudging through sand. Bradley points to a Sphinx next to a pyramid.

"My people built that for me, but it just sits there. All I ever wanted was a friend like you."

The mummy pushes on the side. They walk through a dark corridor and enter a room lit from above. Golden moonlight reveals drawings of Egyptians lining up before a boy with a crown sitting on a black chair. Nuggets of red, green and white sparkle everywhere.

"Nice colors," Bradley says.

"As you can see, there's not much to do here except watch the light change. It gets boring after a few thousand years. I'd invite you to play marbles, but these jewels don't roll."

Bradley eyes the large box on the floor with the life-sized boy carved on top. "Toys?"

"Afraid not. I just wanted you to see my room. I bet yours is more fun."

So they travel back, past the camels, over the clouds and around the world, until they descend again through the trees and into Bradley's bedroom.

The boys stay up all night playing Monopoly. Predictably, little King Tut buys up Boardwalk and Park Place, mortgages all his properties and becomes a tycoon.

Author's Note:
I didn't know what was in the closet when I started to write this in a 20-minute session as part of the writing club where I live in North Carolina. (I'm glad it wasn't a monster! --Aren't you?)

Lucky Charms

Five-year-old Sean was born March 17th and he loved *Lucky Charms*™. On his third birthday while the sun shined on his cereal, the Leprechaun leapt onto the table, danced a jig and took a bow. "I'm Patrick,' he said tipping his top hat. "I'm your new best friend. And boy, do you need me."

Patrick shared all his time with Sean. Whenever Sean played in the sandbox, the Leprechaun would dance atop Sean's castles and sing, "Oh, Danny Boy." On special occasions, he would spray the air with *Pink Hearts* *Yellow Moons* *Orange Stars* and *Green Clovers.*

Most days, Sean's mother was busy working, and his father travelled. Sean played with friends at school, but Patrick was always with him, especially when he had a question or felt down.

At supper, his parents talked about grown up stuff. One night, he asked his mom if she was eating too much meatloaf. She said, "A baby is coming." Sean decided the baby must really like meatloaf. Patrick assured him: "Don't worry. You're the apple of their eye, lad, and after all, you were here first."

Every night after brushing teeth, Sean's mom read him adventure stories and kissed him three times. When the door closed, Patrick always whispered, "Sweet dreams, lad." Sean dreamed of kicking balls, building skyscrapers, and playing policeman. And every day, Patrick would pat him on the back and help him ponder things.

Today when Sean came for breakfast, his mother bent over and struggled for a chair. Sean fetched her purse, and she called a taxi, then his Dad. She told him her "concoctions" were getting close.

When she hung up, she asked for water. Before Sean could hand her the glass, though, it looked like she spilled it on the floor. "Water's breaking," she blurted. Sean froze, but Patrick read his face: "She's still holding the glass, lad, and *you* didn't spill it."

When the taxi came, his mother sat in front and Sean climbed in back. He held the door for Patrick who wanted to crouch on the floor, but Sean made him wear a seatbelt.

"Lakeside Hospital, hurry!" his mother puffed as they sped off. Between puffs, she turned to Sean with a smile. "Today, you'll be my little man. Daddy's on his way, but he might not get here in time, so Grammy will meet us."

Patrick chimed in, "Good, we can all play in the waiting room." No one laughed.

A nurse helped his mom into a wheelchair and pushed her to a bright room on the third floor. After Grammy joined them, he and Patrick played hide-and-seek. But there weren't many places to hide, and his mom moaned a lot.

The moment the doctor stepped in, Grammy stepped out and led them to a waiting room with toys. Before Sean could grab the cherry-topped patrol car, Patrick locked eyes: "You're a big boy now, and soon you'll have company."

"What do you mean?" Sean blinked.

"A baby, I think."

Sure enough, a few hours later, Grammy held Sean up to the window to see rows of babies. Somebody made mistakes with the diaper pins, though: Babies were screaming their teeth out. Grammy pointed to two rosy cheeks in front sleeping soundly. "Those two sleeping beauties are your sisters, Sean. --Twins."

Patrick clicked his heels. "Pretty soon, there'll be so much jabbering in your house, lad, you won't be able to hear me." Waving his wand, he streaked the air with hearts, moons, stars and clovers.

Sean was so busy watching his wriggling sisters he hardly noticed. "Ooh, two!" he squealed, "Two, *Lucky Charms*[1]!"

Author's Note:
I enjoy writing "children's stories for adults" like this. "Lucky Charms" was originally published in *Cape Fear Voices*. (I wrote it as part of Carolina Coastal Writers, a local group where we often draft stories in 20-25 minutes working from a prompt. (It took much longer to finish and polish.)

---

[1]   **Lucky Charms** is a trademark of General Mills IP Holdings II, LLC Delaware.

Puzzle Pieces

A partial picture of serenity.
We always endeavor to run out;
But what if we have too many?

Cinderella and
the Cabbage Prince

The real story about Cinderella might surprise you because Disney sweetened it for Hollywood.

The real Prince grew up in a castle with a vegetable garden on the south side. His parents were both kind, but kind of frumpy. They loved cabbage along with their tubers, especially rutabagas. The young Prince loved it, too, beginning with the aromas from the kitchen as it all stewed.

Like his parents, he developed into an endomorph and could be gassy after a meal. His wit and charm were legendary though and his young face even inspired a line of dolls. Every young maiden in the land wanted the doll if they couldn't have the real Cabbage Prince.

When the Prince was 17, all the maidens who had the wherewithal dressed to the nines and travelled to the castle for the King's debutante ball. Yes, Cinderella was among them. (She preferred to be called Cindy, but her twisted stepsisters never obliged and just wanted their laundry done.)

As you'll recall, before she arrived, the singing bluebirds did a righteous job with her gown and hair. Unfortunately, poor Cindy had been scrubbing the floor all day in her bare feet as she always did, but the birds were so chirpy they forgot to give them the same attention.

You see, Cindy always made a game of dropping bits of cheese all day for the starving mice, and even smaller nibbly bits would find their way underfoot. So let's just say that Cindy cleaned up nicely, but her foot hygiene left something to be desired. And remember the poor girl did leave in a hurry, so she did run barefoot through the garden to the pumpkin and slipped on her high heels in the carriage. Disney leaves that part out.

At the big ball, the Prince danced with most of the maidens, even the stepsisters (who might've been born in a cabbage patch). However, he knew by their argumentative attitudes they were not his type. The dance with Cinderella was nicer than Disney portrays. He wasn't that fond of her perfume, but she had a nice way about her, and he really liked the way her eyes sparkled like the chandeliers. But when the clock struck 12, she kind of came and went, and then there was a big hullabaloo because the ball was over.

Princey was caught flatfooted staring at the chandelier before he realized. He couldn't run fast, and by the time he got to the steps, he only spied the lonely high heel. The moment he held it to his nose, he knew he had to find her. The aroma was intoxicating. He was in love, but somehow couldn't remember her face, only the dazzling chandelier.

That night he slept with her stinky shoe. The next day he set out to find her, stopping at every cottage asking every maiden therein to remove her shoes and socks. After a morning of smelling feet, he lunched on a piece of Swiss and sliced rutabaga. In the afternoon, it was the same story: "No, your feet smell too nice."… "No, too much talcum powder." …"No, your feet smell, but don't smell right."… "No, but nice bunions."

It was near sunset. He and his coachman, not to mention the horses, were getting bushed. Yet a well-appointed cottage on the hill beckoned. The stepmother welcomed him in and introduced the Prince to her two daughters. He didn't recognize them until they started arguing, but to be polite he smelled their feet. They smelled so pretty, he almost gagged. "Sorry you two," he said.

Just then, a bluebird nudged the door to the room where barefooted Cindy was singing. He caught a whiff. The old hag insisted her "cleaning lady' didn't attend the ball, but he demanded she take a seat. Before he even bent over, the Cabbage Prince knew this was his Cinderella stinky foot. He kissed her feet repeatedly and so excessively that it took the coachman and the two sisters some time to pull him away.

Naturally, the stepmother insisted on a handsome sum of gold before she would permit him to marry her. And, not surprisingly, the stepsisters did not wash their feet quite as often or with as much gusto after Cindy left.

Of course, Princey always called her Cindy, and for the record they had five girls all with flat, sweaty feet. The family always ate meals together -- and dined on corned beef and cabbage at least five times a week. That was the secret of why they lived happily ever after.

Author's Note:
When my daughters were about 3 and 7 years old, I would read *Cinderella* at bedtime from one of those condensed books with the cardboard pages. I thought the book too short, so I embellished the story and morphed it into "Cinderella Stinky Foot." We all laughed when I smelled their feet, and yes, they were both princesses. I finally authored the story in 2022, adding the Prince's family history, and read it to my granddaughters at age 5 and 7.

Bunk Bed Brothers

Bunk bed brothers, we chatter into the night
About black magic, nightmares, things unseen
Brave new inventions fast unfurled
So keen – they'll change the world.

Make us famous like Wright and Pine
(As in Kitty Hawk and stop that cough).
Ching-ching! Just can't turn them off,
Ideas so bold and so incredibly fine
Like yours, brother, and especially mine.
Big brother Wally's always gonna know more
"Beaver" kicks from below to even the score.
Sunshine station wagon, seven bound for Jax beach
Superman summer, snapdragon towels for each
Coppertone and coconut waft on a warm breeze
Waiting for that wave rolling big enough to please
Beachballs and bare feet bounce on the sand
Can't touch bottom. Wanna be a man?
Banana bikes and snow cones, garage games and fairs
Basket-weave fences, zip lines, rooftops and dares...

It was meatloaf Mondays from August 'til December
(Or so it seems, that's what I remember.)
And one jealous Christmas, brother beware
(Forget BBs, I got a gun that only shoots air)
"Gotta have one" to Mom you burst, "Me too!"
It's all too much for big brother to chew.
Yet Quick Draw McGraw unwraps it first
You shoot at me -- and I shoot you.

In April, a sun shower stops and bisects our yard
Half in, half out, we flitter back and forth hard
Like laughing ping-pong balls, grass tickling our feet.
The sheet of rain bounces, we race up the street.

*

Whatever became of those clear summer nights
When we sat back-to-back watching starlight
Against that blanket that wraps around all our cares--
The North Star, Orion's Belt, the wandering Bears?
When "Father Knows Best" and God loved us all,
A sky full of fireflies answering the call
And they really did fall – (just like Dad said).
Winding Earthward in the wee hours of the night,
Those strange stars made no sound, put up no fight.
Beneath that Milky cloud a boyhood memory is shroud:
For more than an hour our hearts beat with wonder
Our spirits a-thunder as we counted aloud
Breaking into the hundreds, you and me,
A "moment of being" crystallized for eternity.

Author's Note:

In Jacksonville, Florida, where my family lived for a few years in the mid-'60s, you could sit outside at night in the winter and watch meteor showers in only a jacket.

… During the day, there were frequent rain showers, typically followed by abundant sun. One afternoon, the sheet of rain really did stop in our front yard, and it lingered for a minute before it ran up the street faster than we could catch it.

… On weekends, the seven of us would pile into our Ford station wagon and head for Jacksonville Beach. Lathered with Coppertone, we'd race into the water until we were up to our necks in the lulls. Then we'd spend an hour jumping the 6-8 ft. waves or diving through them.

… At night, while lying in our bunk bed, my brother, Peter (on the bottom), and I would come up with fantastic money-making ideas that kept us up late. (The only invention I can remember now is a catapult to launch garbage cans into the truck.)

… Much later in life, Peter started joking that I was the older brother "Wally" from the TV show, "Leave it to Beaver," which, 'sorta kinda' makes him "The Beave."

Cannonball

A boy's bare feet
Grip granite at river's edge
Sunlight twinkles, and then a cloud
Reveals a form below
He hesitates:
A monster catfish with whiskers
That stretch like tentacles
Waiting to whisk away
Whatever hits the water?
A mermaid with golden hair
Now in a sunbeam touching
Emerald scales of green
and gently beckoning?
The rope swings back to his hands
He leans and decides:
To make a splash!

A Mother's Voice

A lilting lullaby chases away
Lingering chants of schoolyard play,
Claws of lightning and rumbling doubt;
Healing bloody nose, knees and egos,
Soothing hearts from inside out
-- Her voice sends us on our way
With a song to sing, words to recall,
The silent pounding of eagle's wings
Soaring above dark patches and pains
To feel the beauty of it all,
The beat of hope still resounding
Beyond the echoing valley
-- Where love remains

Author's Note:
We all remember the sound of our mother's voice. My mother graduated from The Julliard School of Music, then sang soprano at the Paper Mill Playhouse and folk songs on live radio in New York City with her friend Betty. My mother enjoyed singing all her life. (My Dad sang with her in many church choirs, and they sang together well into their 80s as part of a community chorus in Lee County, NC.) Many who knew my mother called her a "saint," and I would agree. She had a heart for the world, and breathed love and kindness into her family and the community around her. For that I am grateful.

The Catholic Years

First Confession:

I don't remember this second-grader's obsession,
But I do recall the 'Sin of All' in that dark procession
-- My class and me as we sniggered and grinned
When wild-eyed Frankie McGrew first went in:

Instead of kneeling and bearing all contrite feeling
He repeatedly tapped that electric, velvet kneeler.
What he (heatedly) whispered to Father McKeilor
-- Or more likely vice-versa -- we never knew.
But in the "occupied" light outside that abode
McGrew keyed out a *distress* in Morris Code.

We'd think back on that S.O.S. as long as we'd live.
And that day, as our class sang from the hymnal
We wondered if God would ever forgive
The boy who tapped that ambiguous signal --
Or if the knees of us in line He'd buckle
To chance such a time as this to chuckle.

Author's Note:
This poem is based on an event at my first confession with my second-grade
class in New Jersey. --The names have been changed to protect the guilty.

For the uninitiated about Catholic confession: At the back of the church is the
confessional. The priest sits in a room just big enough for his chair. His room is
flanked by two small rooms each with a cushioned kneeler, and he slides open
a cloth screen when it's your turn to confess. But here's the important part for
this poem anyway: The kneeler activates a light to let those waiting in line know
the room is occupied.

First Communion:

The Lord did enter my soul that day
A spirit of warmth way down south:
I thanked the Lord for everything;
He stuck to the roof of my mouth.

Altar Boys:

"Et cum spiritu tuo"
The altar boys understand
But not the congregation, no, no

Until the tables turn around
Changing '60s Mass to celebration
(More restrained than unbound)
With acoustic guitar and wind-song band
"I once was lost, but now am found"
Ergo, in English, in cassock and surplice
Marching straight ahead with candlesticks
"Thou shalt not falter" during procession

At the altar, one good boy lights the wicks
(The other rattles congregation with sound)
We boys always pray for sermons with reason and rhyme
No fiery bricks or demons -- and shorter than last time

We ring the bells and pushbutton chimes
With reverent precision at appointed times
We genuflect, bow, kneel, sit and stand
Again kneel, kneel forever, until communion
Then finally the band:
And in one voice communal we sing
For freedom the blessed recessional
(More temporal than eternal)

But after Mass, in the sacristy
Once or twice there is a travesty:
One altar boy faints, losses his breakfast
Another chugs spirits of priestly wine
He thinks it's all a blast and feels fine.
I was the only one who ever knew:
I never told, but shhhhhhhhh --
it wasn't Frankie McGrew.

Author's Note:
When I first became an altar boy in 1964, the Catholic Mass was still in Latin. We used both bell ringers and push-button chimes that could play exactly four notes. Although I did faint once after Mass, it was another boy who enjoyed the spirits. I was dumbfounded and said so. But as he told me, "What happens in the sacristy stays in the sacristy."

Confirmation:

Think Catholic catechism times ten
with 6th graders freaking about public speaking.
Rote memory would come in handy
When Archbishop Ben would preside
With questions, no one could hide.

Certainly, it'd be just one Jim Dandy
If I was the one struggling inside
Who blanched and had to confide
Rather dreamily to the Holy assembly:

"Ahem, Ahem...." (here comes a gem)...
"Rather than respond directly to what the Bishop poses
After such an enlightening sermon, so bold and so frank,
I'd just like to thank all of you, and mention I studied hard, too.

Yet what is now so plain in front of everyone's noses
This simple question I blew 'cause I just drew a blank."

There'd be laughter, of course
Then I'd have to saddle that horse
And ride it all the way from here to graduation.
My classmates would get but a slap on the chin
Confirmed so they could move up and in.
But if I miss on this, my spirit would be left back
The butt of an endless joke and teen attack,

Yes, I knew my stuff, but it did get chilly
When Bishop Ben first called my friend Billy

(Downright chilly for him I mean).
Yet he answered faster'n I'd ever seen
More precisely than with charm.
Bishop Ben seemed satisfied though.
As for me, I never had to go
But I did get uncomfortably warm.

Then I got slapped on the cheek with all the rest
The one who knew the answers backwards and best.
But thank God I was never taken to task
For that question I was never asked.

Author's Note:

I originally wrote this in 2012, recalling my confirmation in 1966. The Bishop would visit our church in the Spring and after a long sermon ask a handful of questions selecting victims at random. We needed to memorize answers to 30 pages of questions. It was a daunting task, and when the time came, we were all expected to raise our hands. (Some did so more enthusiastically than others.) But the hardest part was waiting to see who "won" this reverse lottery.

There were about 60 of us and fortunately only half a dozen questions. After the Q&A we all knelt at the altar, waiting for the Bishop to tap us on the cheek. The "slap" is symbolic of the "hard knocks" Christians may face in life, though this is not verbatim from my catechism.

Show-and-Tell

Zack attends a kindergarten for the gifted, and today it is thunder storming for Show-and-Tell. He thought about bringing his inflatable dragon but knew it would take too long to blow up. So he went with his mother's idea: A shoebox. She told him there was a Greek god inside, not to open it until his turn, and remember her words.

The classroom air is filled with anticipation, and smells uncomfortably moist from rubber boots, dripping umbrellas and damp jackets hanging on pegs. The children are sitting in a circle, and Mrs. Marten is calling on them one at a time. Zack is sitting next to Ned, who lives next door.

"Do you want to go first, Ned?" Mrs. Marten asks.

Coincidentally, Ned pulls a purple plastic dragon out of his lunchbag and flies it around the room saying, "Grrr, grrr, zoom-zoom, *Zooooom.*" He soars it by Doreen's face, and says, "You better behave, or I'll burn you."

Zack blurts, "*My* dragon can do that."

Mrs. Marten jumps in, "OK, Ned. We got the idea. You can sit down now."

Frank takes a giant *Lego* Ferris wheel out of a box and announces: "This is *mine.*" He turns it on, but the wheel only goes around once before squeaking to a stop. He switches the toggle back and forth until he panics and breaks into tears.

"Crybaby," Zack whispers. Ned snickers.

"Let's let Doreen go."

Doreen holds up a blonde-haired doll with blue eyes, dressed only in a diaper. "It wets and cries," she says. The baby starts wailing and moving its head and eyes. "That's what she does when she's wet." Doreen changes the baby, and it stops crying.

Next Larry goes, waving his "Empire Strikes Back" light saber around the room, saying, "Vooom-vooom, vooom-vroom. Die Darth Vader, die!"

"Can I go next?" asks a waving Eddie. He produces an emergency beacon. "This is what you do if your car breaks down." He flips up a yellow reflector and turns on a siren. Everyone covers their ears. Then he turns on the strobe until Doreen appears to be going into a seizure.

So what's in your box, Mrs. Marten finally asks Zack, "shoes?"

"I'm not sure I should open it, " Zack replies.

"Why not?"

'There's a Greek god inside, but maybe you'll think it's nothing."

"Let's see," she says. The class echoes.

Zack pulls the top off and shows everyone the box is empty.

"What's it say on the bottom?" Mrs. Marten wants to know.

"'Shoes,' I think. My mom wrote it."

"No, it says 'Zeus.' He was a Greek god."

"*You* said it, not me."

Lightning cracks outside, a branch strikes the window, and all the children react. The overhead lights flicker, then the bulbs pop like *Jiffy-Pop*. The kids shriek. Ned is hugging his dinosaur, Doreen's doll is crying, the Ferris wheel is spinning fast, Larry's light saber is *vroom-vrooming*, and the strobe starts flashing again.

The wall clock advances to 2:59 pm. Mrs. Marten is stunned, genuinely concerned she might morph into a toad. "Maybe you should put him back in the box now," she offers gently.

"OK, but my mom said to ask one thing first."

"What's that?"

"Where do you keep *your* god?"

Author's Note:
This is a "children's story for adults" that I drafted a few years ago as part of Carolina Coastal Writers in about 25 minutes. (The cartoon took much longer.) It seems like a children's story, but a serious question, and its unwritten corollaries, live inside the box.

Sister Mary Judas Roars

Her name was Sister Mary Judas;[2] the students called her 'Scariot.' She was the red-faced principal of our Florida elementary school in the '60s whose most relaxed expression was a scowl. Her nun's habit dripped with resentment, and the white flag at her forehead was not a sign of surrender.

When she wasn't scouring the halls looking for someone to devour, we imagined she blasted steam out of her head like Tom Terrific. Celibacy must be hell. Why does a woman become a nun? Is it an act of love or contrition, or more likely, revenge?

Once at lunch, two tough boys squirted ketchup on each other and broke into a fistfight. A teacher pulled them apart, but strangely they weren't sent to the principal's office. Five minutes after lunch though, Sister Mary Judas stood in the doorway of our 6th grade class glaring. She summoned one of the pugilistic boys to the front. Bending him over the teacher's desk, she beat him with a stick until he whimpered and cried. The other boy met a similar fate, and they both spent the afternoon in front of the class sitting in trash cans.

At 8:35 one morning, Sister Mary Judas broke in over the PA fulminating: A boy in uniform had heaved a rock from an overpass and struck a car, narrowly missing the windshield and inflicting $1,750 in damage. Waves of anger vibrated the wall speaker. The guilty boy was too terrified to confess. --That day I promised never to find myself in Scariot's crosshairs.

Early one December, our class went to a matinee of "The Robe," which followed the robe-winning soldier after the crucifixion. At the end, the Romans filled our (now) Christian hero with arrows.

---

[2]   *Not her real name*

For me, it was worse: I'd been sitting on a wad of *Bazooka* gum for two hours.

Surprisingly, in the rush to leave, no one noticed the pink Rorschach on my butt. It was a long ride back to school though, and when I rose from the seat of my classmate's station wagon, a gooey string stretched lugubriously behind. I tiptoed away and wrapped a sweater around my waist.

Arriving back to class last, I alerted the teacher to my predicament. She sent me to the principal's office. The secretary directed me to the nurse's room; the nurse was out, but I should wait. My stomach jumped on a trampoline. A dark form finally appeared in the doorway, then flew in. The raven was not smiling. "Take your pants off," she said.

I tried to stall: "Why?"

She roared at me. I was now in such a hurry I couldn't wrestle my pants over my shoes. She watched, then screeched--*"Take your shoes off first!"* This maneuver prolonged the agony. (That I had donned underwear without moth holes that day was no consolation.)

Topping things off, there was a freezer in the chilly room. The nun popped a cube from the ice tray and showed me how to rub it fast to harden the gum and pick it off. My brain taunted: "You're standing next to Scariot in your *Fruit of the Looms*." She left after the demo, but *Bazooka* is tenacious. Eventually, she returned to see my sticky situation, and said they'd call home. My mother didn't drive, so I wasn't sure how this movie would end. Yet 47 minutes later, a taxi arrived with a clean pair of pants.

Thinking back on it, I realize now that Sister Mary Judas may have roared like a lion, but there was probably a kitten under the hood.

COMING ATTRACTIONS!

The movie my classmates could never see.

Author's Note:
This story is based on true events and was nominated for a *Cape Fear Voices* humor award. It is my favorite cartoon so far.

Hailey's Comet

First she's cold, then she's hot.
She wants to play all Saturday
Every week, at my house --
Sword fights, fastball, poker and slapjack.
She's the meow, I am the mouse.

In Monopoly, Hailey's the banker.
Waves 'Park Place' in my face;
I just want to spank her.
She's the Riverboat Queen,
Keeps the token; my ears are smokin.'
Afterwards it's video games.
Ten minutes in, she puts it down;
The controller's all broken.

Why does Hailey have to be so mean?

Mom says she's a tomboy, likes to play the guy.
Any boy tries to kiss her, likes to get a black eye.
Get mad and pull her hair? --Don't you even dare!
She'll put you in a head lock, tie you in a chair.
She likes to watch boys squiggle and squirm.
Coughs in your face 'til you pick up a germ.

"Cry Uncle?" she'll ask in wolverine mask.
She takes it off and then switches tack:
Time to make a splice
Of forgiveness and play nice.

She lets you go with a smile,
A wisp that doesn't last awhile.
It's a smile from the cat's meow to the mice.
It's a comet that lasts a fleeting moment, heaven sent.
(Now you know the definition of "evanescent.")
For a comet with a tail is not a star with a twinkle,

She relishes terror, my blood she wants to sprinkle.

She lures me outside; it sounds like relief.
But she's Frankenstein's Bride, a gangster, a thief:
"I'll be Bonnie & Clyde, you be the police."
"Now it's time for a little fun," she says with a grin.
"You -- RUN!"

Prefilled and premeditated, it's a Bazooka water gun
And she never for a moment hesitated:
Pumps the barrel 1, 2, 3, then points the thing at me.
"It's scalding hot," she says, as I stumble and flee.

Hailey cackles, giving another pump,
Pulls the trigger, roasting my rump.
I moan out loud, and she just laughs,
"This gun's a gas, it's so-o keen."

Why does Hailey have to be so mean?

I round the corner and into the house,
Lock all the doors and cower like a mouse.
From behind the curtain I steal a quick peek.
She's gloating by the door with a thin black grin,
Plotting 100 ways to get herself back in.
"Mom," I cry with a desperate shriek,
"Does she really have to come back next week?"

"You know the answer. I'll give you a minute,
Then open the door, and let her back in it…
Hailey's mom and me go way back, you know.
Before her Roger and your father, Roy,
I must confess, I, too, was a tomboy.
So, no, I don't like to see my son always cryin.'
What kind of man will you be: A mouse or a lion?"

So 'Hailey the Comet' sashays into the kitchen.
She gets quiet awhile as we eat Chicken Lickin.'
Then Mom and Hailey start to giggle and chatter
About school, shoes, and stuff that doesn't matter.
Finally, the buzzer goes off on the oven for 'bake.'
Out comes a cherry pineapple upside-down cake.
We all eat a fat slice and lick our plates clean.

Why does Hailey have to be so-o mean?

Is she cool or is she not?
Embroidered blue jeans,
Sweater, pink and green,
Strawberry hair, fragrance of spice.
Hailey smiles now, ruby lips, no ice.
"I like your mom," she says, locking my eyes,
"Really, just so you know, between us guys."

At the door, this time Hailey doesn't flick my ears.
Rather with a wink, her finger slides down my nose.
But I'm deep sixing my fears, and it's time she knows.
Quick-drawing my finger and looking her in the eye,
Says I with a grin: "I'll catch *you* next week --.
And just so you know, I'm not talking Hide & Seek."

Author's Note:
When I authored this poem in 2010, I decided to make it about pre-teens, but here's what inspired it: When I was in first grade in New Jersey, a neighbor-friend, my age, was a girl nicknamed "I-I." She also came from a family of seven and our families were close. Although all girls still had cooties, it seemed OK in my mind because everyone said she was a tomboy, including her. She liked to wrestle (as often as I would allow) – yet she would eventually pin me. (Her older brothers taught her well.) Still, I didn't always allow, and it grew old. Fortunately, we moved to Florida before I suffered any lasting damage, and by high school I knew better than to join the wrestling team.

Red Hots

Geoffrey O'Hara loved *Red Hots*[3].® He was an Irish boy in the 6th grade with red hair and face a creamy white. Shirley, who sat in front of him, said he had so many freckles it looked like he bumped into a spray gun. Her bouncing red curls menaced him, and he'd sometimes flick her locks with his pen until she would tell him to stop.

His best friend, Robert, teased him for years that he liked Shirley, but Geoffrey always denied it. They both knew she had had cooties which wasn't something you could get over overnight.

As the youngest with three sisters and a 17-year-old brother, Geoffrey craved attention. But his sisters dominated his mother's time. So ever since Robert moved next door, they had become fast friends. After school, they'd often walk to the candy store. Robert bought sourballs and Butterfingers, but Geoffrey only bought Red Hots. He'd eat so many sometimes, it looked like lipstick.

Robert knew Geoffrey would do anything to get them. So now that they were starting 7th grade, Robert upped the ante for what

---

[3]   *Red Hots* is a trademark of Ferrara Candy Company, Chicago, Illinois.

the boys at school called "The Big Red Dare." They all cringed with delight, and soon Robert stockpiled enough Red Hots to fill a gallon jug.

Friday at recess, the boys enticed Geoffrey with visions of the cinnamon nuggets until he drooled. Then they sprang it: If he could kiss Shirley in the next 10 days, they'd give him 1,000 "rubies."

Wasting no time, Geoffrey stopped by Shirley's table at lunch and offered her a few. When she refused, he smiled and gave her one of the boxes from his lunch bag. She managed to smile and then shared them with her friends. But in the afternoon, he tapped her shoulder and handed her a note: "What movie do you want to see?" She crumpled it.

He thought about Shirley all weekend. At lunch Monday, he offered her Red Hots again. Her friends tittered when she politely said 'no.' Walking away, he heard, "He has the hots for you."

Tuesday, he detected more of a smile in her refusal. Shirley's friends teased again about "the hots." This time, Geoffrey turned with a grin, "I do indeed."

As he took his seat Wednesday, the smell of strawberry shampoo arrested his brain. His note: "Your hair smells yummy ;-) My brother will drive us." Shirley folded it in half.

At lunch Thursday, he winked when she said 'no.' In history, a light went on. He jotted: "What kind of candy do YOU like?"

She scribbled: "Almond Joy."

Friday, he gave her the Almond Joy at lunch and left Red Hots for the table. His afternoon note: "What about West Side Story Sat. @ 8?"

Shirley's note back: "YES."

Geoffrey's brother offered pointers before the movie. Geoffrey slipped his arm over her shoulder after she finished her candy bar. They held hands for a while, and again on the way home in the backseat. On her doorstep, Shirley told him she had "a very nice time." They gazed into each other's eyes, and their lips touched softly like frosting on a strawberry cupcake. Shirley said he tasted like Red Hots and suggested they do it again sometime.

"Maybe next weekend," he replied.

Geoffrey collected the jug of Red Hots the next day. On Monday, he and Shirley chattered on the steps at recess; the first lovebirds in their class. The boys huddled around Robert. He didn't have to say it but did: They wouldn't need to dare Geoffrey to kiss Shirley anymore. In that moment, they all knew their futures had changed, and the implications triggered warm, tingly feelings. Robert passed out sourballs, another boy, M&Ms. They popped candy into their mouths and, one by one, glanced at the girls giggling nearby as if for the first time.

Author's Note:
When I wrote the closing scene for this story, I pictured myself on the playground of my middle school in Plymouth, N.C. After it was first published in a Valentine's edition of *Cape Fear Voices*, a friend told me the story brought back memories from her school years. …Maybe it will do the same for you.

I Am the Hare

Out of the gate
and into thin air
With lightning
speed I own
the lead
Don't see anyone
anywhere

Skies drool
like blueberry
marmalade
Everyone knows
I've got it made
For I am the hare--
Out of the glen and into the shade

Author's Note:
While "The Tortoise & the Hare" is taught as a cautionary tale about complacency, did you ever stop to identify with the hare?

I wrote this in 2010 during the Great Recession. I realized I lived much of my life in the fast lane. Sometimes I was too busy (or having too much fun) doing what I did best to take breaks. There were always deadlines, of course. Yet while I was working, I never felt I had it "made in the shade." At the time, I was searching for better employment, so I had to keep going, but I did stop to jot this story down.

Perhaps, Simon & Garfunkel's lyrics say it best: "Slow down, you move too fast / You've got to make the morning last." And maybe the turtle should win once in a while. (Just not on my watch.)

The Spitball that Missed

Splat!

Frank never missed. He could dot an 'i' on the blackboard from the back row of his 6th grade history class, no problem. But today was different: It was April Fool's Day, and Sammy had slapped Frank on the back just as he was about to launch the slippery wad from his *Bic Special.*

There was a collective gasp as the ball slid down the lens of Mr. Gruff's horn-rimmed glasses. The wooly-haired teacher stood aghast, his face a ripening tomato. Finally, he took a breath and barked: "Frank, come up here!"

Head down, Frank took a sideways glance at the clock as he baby-stepped up to Mr. Gruff's desk. Just then, the 3 o'clock bell rang. The class said a silent prayer for him as they left.

"Now, why did you hit me with that spitball, boy?" Mr. Gruff snapped, his nose scrunching up like he had to eat a rutabaga.

"Well...I really didn't *mean* to, sir. You see, Sammy slapped my back just as it was coming out the barrel."

"This stops today!" Mr. Gruff snarled. "Now, let me have it."

Reluctantly, Frank pulled the *Bic* from his pocket. Mr. Gruff waved it like a dagger and whipped it into the trash with a clang. Then he grabbed his birch paddle and glared at the boy. "You can either take five licks right now – *or-r-r,* you can stay after school and do something for me."

Frank paused to consider his options. Experience told him five licks would sting a while. "Yes, sir, whatever it is, I'll do it."

"Take a seat," Mr. Gruff growled. He set an empty shoebox on the desk and then slapped down a stack of yellow paper. "Fill that box with spitballs -- and you don't leave until it's full, ya hear?"

Frank nodded. He started tearing paper and loading pieces into his mouth until his cheeks bulged. He pumped out spitballs like cookie dough. Once the bottom of the box was covered, he started making the balls bigger. His mouth became parched, his tongue sticky. He desperately wanted a drink, but the water fountain was down the hall. He pressed on, one yellow ball at a time.

At 3:53 p.m., he deposited the soggy box on Mr. Gruff's desk. "All done, sir. Filled to the brim."

Mr. Gruff took the box and dropped it into the trash with a thud, then looked at Frank squarely in the eye. "Now, I want you to promise me, son, you'll never make another spitball in my class!"

"Yes sir," he quickly responded. "I'll never make another *spitball* in your class again."

Mr. Gruff pointed to the door: "Now go."

Just outside, the boy cracked the cover of his history book where he had placed a carefully folded airplane.

Frank's laughter bounced off the walls as he ran down the hallway. He knew he had hit Mr. Gruff right in the nose.

An important history lesson.

Author's Note:

I wrote this story in my 20s but lost it and recreated it for *Cape Fear Voices.* Although it's fiction, it was inspired by a retiring teacher. One day, "Mr. Gruff" (not his real name) wanted us to watch a filmstrip on Sir Walter Raleigh and proceeded to thread the spool and flick on the projector. He asked a boy to turn out the lights and then made his way back to his desk where he became engrossed in the newspaper. Meanwhile, the class was not focused on the history unfolding on the screen, but rather on the celluloid piling up on the floor. The sprawling mess was a yard wide before a merciful student called it to his attention.

Thin Ice

Steel teeth chisel ice to pick up speed
Melting parallel lines, once then twice
Yearning to be free, a bucking steed…

The crisscrossing of blades sounds so nice
Slipping 'cross this span of frozen lace,
The sun mirrors while the skates go slice

His perfect Sunday is now in place
Arms in cadence to push and to glide
Clouds give way to sunshine in his face

Blades cutting hard, send shards side to side

*

In motion,
Though it's certainly true
Bodyweight can spread and hide
Beneath the cold winter sky so blue

But there's something else you should know:
From left foot to right is not much time
For skaters to sense an impending crime

Boy, listen more to the sheet beneath
It sings a song as you glide along
A song to match air, but with more teeth

He chugs along with a huff and puff
Starts to listen, struggling inside
Fissures zig, spit and zag, no bluff

Now let me confide,
As the morning sun rises so grand
It works patiently from above and below
With the sound of an out-of-tune band

Ice stretches like the call of the wild
Yet below, the temperature grows mild
A crying child no longer napping

*

But, boy,
Skating's fast fun, so alive and awake!
And for a heavy kid set on candy,
The ice's a gift, a shortcut to take.

Oh what a day so bright and dandy
On the other side, around the bend
There's the candy aisle at the 5 &10.

Clark bars, Baby Ruths and M&Ms!
There's something here you don't comprehend?

That morning before he left the house:
"Dress for the weather my toy soldier."
His mama just couldn't help but grouse.

Blades shining over his shoulder,
Mama's marine is only 13.
Last night was clear and the lake did freeze,
But outside it's going to 37 degrees.

Chugging along, his sweet tooth calls *"Please"*
He's skating now from home to heaven
"Skittles for me, forget Charles Dickens!"

He's listening to ice, plink plinking along
Thinking, "Why didn't I invite Kevin?"...
The ice is off key, one note's all *wrong*

To slow any further would spell doom
He maintains momentum, hopes for best
(Ice monsters suck kids like a vacuum)

Yet his heart melts to wax in his chest
Stepping again, hears groaning behind
The faster he goes, the lighter he gets.

The shore lies ahead if skates can find
Ice monster can't catch me now, he thinks
But there's moaning, and sun strikes him blind

He steps two, three four, stops and blinks
He's all sweaty, but the panic subsides
Finally ashore, he checks armor for chinks

Carefully, he slings blades across his back
Marching forward, glad to be alive
And finally back on his one true tack.

Yet looking back at the lake he traversed
He knows for sure it might've been worse:

Thirty yards from shore, I swear, no more
A gaping hole could have taken him
Hook, line and sinker, right down the bore

Monster would devour him limb by limb
(Certainly that would be a stinker)
The boy wondered why and what for?

He walked away, turned at the blinker
Considering his life for a while.
' Course, he's not really a big thinker

(In his mouth, he chokes back bile)
Soon it hits like rock candy 'tween the eyes:
"--There's no time in life to hesitate

"For girls and certainly not for us guys
Just carry a reason to survive some more."
-- Then his mind shifts back to the store."

*

So he rounds the bend avoiding a stumble.
"Time to get that taste out of my mouth.
My stomach is starting to grumble!"

"I deserve a special treat," he thought
"A malted shake with cherry on top!
--Not just M&Ms for all I fought.-

He savors a Hershey border to border
Then swallows M&M's one by one
Green, red and blue -- in that order.

Tall glass arrives with a flourish for fun
He takes a spoon to savor the whipped cream
There's no one there, he's the only one

He stirs, then slurps his chocolate dream
Until the long straw at the bottom makes
That "all gone" sound of all empty shakes

Last he takes the cherry by the stem
That has been waiting on his napkin
And swallows it, slowly lowering it in.

He wipes off the dribble from his chin
Burps quite satisfied, then swipes the change
He counts it carefully, surprised to find

No, the change from a ten, it's not strange
It comes to two dollars seventy-nine.
Enough to buy more bubble gum, whoo-hoo!

This will all work out just perfectly fine
Better than non-pareils or *JuJuBes*®[4]
A month's worth of gum will all be mine.

He leaves a dime to cover the fees
Picks up his skates, and is homeward bound

*

Where street meets the lake, a boat's run aground
A sign not to make the same mistake.
"This time, I'll take the long way around."

When he gets home, his mother's voice quakes:
"Wanna catch a death? she said, 'Wear your hat!'"
He takes it in stride, knows what it takes.

"I love you, Mom," he says, "and that's that."
A nice reply from soldier boy dandy.
--"And your expedition to the store?"

"It was fine as sweet-and-sour candy."
Blowing a big bubble on command,
He drops a sour ball into her hand.

The bubble gets bigger 'n' bigger,
Then pops.
"Next time, Mom," he says, "I'll wear my hat."

Author's Note:
There is a lake in the middle of my hometown in Bergen County, N.J., that separated our house from the shopping center. When my family first moved there in 1970, the lake would regularly freeze over, and the ice could build to eight inches thick. Everyone, young and old, skated on it. However, it was not always as safe as it appeared. The ice could creak when it felt the weight of a skater, and if the ice were thin enough, long cracks could spider outward. Some years later, a boy fell through, and that was the last year of ice skating.

---

[4]   JUJUBES is a trademark of Farley's & Sathers Candy Company, Inc.

Waking Nightmare

Jeremy Fischer tried the backdoor to the farmhouse. To our surprise, it opened. My younger brother, Will, and I were new in town, and we looked up to Jeremy. At 17, he was three years older than me. Jeremy was adopted, an only child, imaginative and intense. Plus, he always knew things we didn't. We weren't sure why Jeremy liked us, but we liked his style and followed his cordovan boots into adventure.

We were glad to move out of the sun, but the dim kitchen trapped the heat. The lights didn't work. Our eyes were drawn to particles dancing in a shaft of sunlight. (Funny how you don't notice the dust surrounding you.) As our eyes adjusted, floorboards peeked through the linoleum. Gazing up, cobwebs came to life; a black widow watched and waited.

We opened all the cabinets, finding ceramic plates and glasses; in the refrigerator, nothing but foggy jars and black yogurt. On the door hung a bank calendar, August 1961--exactly 7 years ago. It entranced Jeremy. Eyes wide, he told us about a runaway teen named Jimmy Rhodes who disappeared in May of '61. "Some say he became a drifter. Others say he must've stopped somewhere or was kidnapped."

Will and I shuddered, then quickly shuffled into the den. Jeremy patted the frayed couch which gave off a cloud of dust and a lingering odor. In the bedroom, a mattress sagged inside a broken frame. As we tiptoed upstairs, a diving pigeon brushed my cheek.

The master bedroom featured a hole in the ceiling, a cracked mirror and a white-spattered quilt. across the bed. At the desk, a typewriter beckoned. Jeremy pulled the sheet and read aloud:

Dear Sylvia,

Why did you leave? Or is that the question you want me to answer? Bad farms make bad marriages. But did we always have to argue until somebody bled? Seven bad years wasn't my fault--just one too many for you. You could never forget or forgive when we was short. Did you forget we both wanted a son? I never blamed you, so why couldn't you accept when our fortune arrived?

Jeremy noticed it wasn't signed. He paused to ponder. "The husband must've given up when the banks foreclosed. But what was their fortune that Sylvia couldn't accept? Did he rob a bank, or did an unfortunate teen step into a hurricane here?"

In the basement, dust layered everything; mildew hung in the air. Jeremy wondered if Jimmy Rhodes' spirit might also be hanging there. We were drawn to a workbench with old tools. Next to it stood a tarnished tablesaw with rough-cut blade. Jeremy thought he noticed dark red on the teeth. Will and I leaned in and confirmed the smears.

We scrambled upstairs and out the back. When Will and I started to run, Jeremy called, "Stop." We didn't want to attract attention, so we walked in silence. After a while, Jeremy said we really didn't know what happened there. If we called the police, we'd get in trouble for trespassing, or worse. He made us swear never to tell another soul.

The thought of that whirring sawblade plagued our sleep for years. Was there really a Jimmy Rhodes? Turns out that was true. As for the rest, we got shined. Jeremy Fischer got a full scholarship and became a professor of literature at UNC. Last year, he published a mystery novel, *Waking Nightmare.*

Author's Note:
In the late '60s, there was an abandoned farmhouse across the highway from where I lived in Plymouth, N.C., a town of about 6,000 where nearly everyone worked for the papermill. The farmhouse enjoyed a certain allure for me, my brother Pete and a young friend. To be sure, the story is fiction. Yet after I put it on paper, it occurred to me that I, an occasional teller of tall tales, could be the real Jeremy Fisher.

My Friend's in the Mob

When I moved to New Jersey from rural North Carolina in the middle of 9th grade in 1970, it was a culture shock. I went from a school where all the guys wore straight legs to one where everyone wore bellbottoms. I went from myopic N.C. history to a world history class so boring the kid behind me spent every day doing math, figuring the markup on a pound of weed if he cut it with oregano.

At lunch in 10th grade, I sat with a friend named Ed* and his heavyset friend, Alberto Garza,* a half-Italian, half-Guatemalan mix. Halfway through his Fritos, Ed whispers to me, "Alberto's father is in the mob." This piqued my curiosity. Alberto was a stubby guy with tinted glasses and a bandana. He looked tough but I figured him for a peach, so I had to ask: "What's it like having a father in the mob?"

"Where'dja hear that?"

"Ed told me."

"What's Ed know?"

"A lot, I think."

"We can't talk about it here."

I asked him if his Dad ever whacked someone.

"Shut up. I'm serious!-- Bad things can happen to people who can't keep their mouths shut. -- *Capiche*?"

So I invited Alberto to my house to play chess, and he was almost as good as me. But when I brought it up again, he didn't want to talk about it.

The next week he invited me to his house. His older brother wasn't home, but I met his Guatemalan mother who spoke broken English. After I beat Alberto at chess again, we visited his basement. He shows me his weights and brags he can bench 200 pounds. "Wanna try?"

"Nah," I said.

"Hah," he sniffs, "I bet you can't bench 60 lbs." I let it go.

Next, he wanted to show me a few things in his bedroom upstairs. He opened his closet and pulled out nunchucks. "Stand back," he says, swinging the weapon under each arm and across his body. "Know what these are?"

He informed me that oak nunchucks can break bones like twigs. Alberto claimed he could snap arms as skinny as mine with his bare hands. I didn't doubt it but couldn't help but smile 'because I knew he never would. 'Wheredja get 'em?"

"My dad gave them to me for Christmas."

Next, Alberto pulled out a BB gun. I chuckled and reminded him I'm 14 and from the Tar Heel state, so there's a 16-gauge Remington pump in my bedroom closet for small game. I suspect his Dad doesn't hunt squirrels. "Does he use the nunchucks or a gun? --Let me guess, a 9 mm Baretta?"

Alberto assured me the nunchucks were his, but his Dad does deal with "squirrels" from time to time. To answer more fully, he pulls out a Billy club and starts slapping it into his palm. "You can do a lot of damage with one of these. Fits in your jacket. It's great for kneecaps -- and late payers."

I know what he means, but I love the chase: "Late payers?"

"Yeah, sometimes store owners gotta pay for protection. Know what I mean?"

"What kinda protection?"

"You know, Chuckie, we gotta lotta rough neighborhoods in Jersey -- Newark, Jersey City...Camden's the worst. Wanna feel safe? Smart store owners pay for a little protection."

"And if they get squirrely?"

"Bad things can happen in bad neighborhoods–slashed tires, broken windows, burglaries, fires. God forbid something happens to your family. That's life. You might say my Dad's in the insurance business." Alberto smiles.

Well, for me, compared to rural N.C., suburban New Jersey was a tough neighborhood. My southern accent was such a lightning rod when I arrived some classmates nearly wet their pants. ...And I sincerely sucked at softball. Yeah, I could've used protection, and as time went on, there was an expanding list of knees to dream about:

- On my first day of gym class, a boy who sat out sick (allegedly) robbed my locker. (I did not see him and had no proof.)
- A troubled teen on my street stole the rare coins I'd been saving since I was seven. (I confronted him and got the coins back. Fifteen years later I visited him in jail.)
- Sophomore year, the JV basketball team turned strange. After I was the first one cut in tryouts, the coach asked me to manage the team. I said 'yes.' What I didn't know: The team wanted their mascot, a diminutive kid who they said I screwed when I accepted the position.
- Junior year, my trigonometry teacher nearly failed me the first quarter. I couldn't understand imaginary numbers, where 'i' equals the square root of negative one. (I transferred from the pre-calculus class to the one where they dotted i's with spitballs.)
- My senior year, a pal stole the girl I had taken to the junior prom.

Of course, I never asked Alberto for protection, and on busboy wages couldn't afford it. So I suffered the taunts, rip-offs, dashed hopes and shattered hearts like everyone else who ever attended high school. (And I also broke some hearts.)

Late one Friday night, me, Ed, Alberto, and another friend who drove got hauled to the police station for--get this--having a BB gun in the trunk. (For the record, I was wearing my purple bell bottoms.) When my Dad picked me up, I reminded him about the 16-gauge pump in my closet, even if we hadn't gone huntin' yet in Jersey. He reminded me, we weren't in North Carolina anymore.

Epilogue: *I never met Alberto's Dad. He did arrive home early the afternoon I visited, and I was ushered out the back door (never to return). I fell out of touch with Alberto, or more likely vice versa. I know he always longed to work in the family business, yet I was never sure how well a Guatemalan-looking Italian would fare. Still, I sometimes imagine him in a swanky pizza parlor somewhere in Camden, oven opened wide, doing what he likes doing best: Selling insurance.*

* Not real names

Family Spring Break, Anyone?

When you're 14 years old, where would you go on Spring Break if you had a choice: The Grand Canyon? Disneyland? Atlantic City? For my family, the answer was "West Virginia," not because any of us kids wanted to go there, but because that's where my parents wanted us to go, and my Dad had veto power.

There may be parts of West Virginia that are nice, but this was 1970 and we were headed on a mission trip to Appalachia, coal country. It was a long day's journey from N.J., and we weren't going to stay at a Holiday Inn or even a Motel 6, but at a Catholic monastery–with real monks.

We knew there would be other families there on this adventure. Yet we had no idea what we would be doing, except that we were there to help people. The accommodations were not stellar. The mattresses and pillows were flat and lumpy, but at least I did not have to sleep in the loft of the barn like some of my siblings.

We were curious about the Brothers. They wore brown robes with ropes around their waists, and were apparently well fed. We all ate dinner in the basement, equipped with kitchen, dining room, and lounge. The Brothers loved regaling the adults with their stories. After the meal, they headed upstairs, saying they would share our assignment in the morning.

Meanwhile, the rest of the adults chattered in the kitchen and did the dishes with no fuss. Some dried with a towel over their shoulders, others put dishes away. We kids mostly watched, glad that no one asked us. (We learned the next night that they were just setting an example.)

In the morning, someone opened a 5-gallon bucket of red paint and distributed it with 4-inch brushes so we could paint the barn. This seemed a monumental task, and it didn't look like we were really helping anyone but the monks who were nowhere to be found. (I suggested rollers, but the nearest hardware was 45 miles away.)

We painted for several days and finished Thursday afternoon. When it rained Friday, we heard that March was still the monastery's slow season, and they didn't field many requests for help.

In the evenings, after dishes, our group of eight kids played Crazy-Eights religiously until bedtime. On Thursday night, two Brothers joined us, squeezing in from either end of the booth. They said if we could play Crazy Eights, we could easily learn their new game called Screw Your Neighbor. It was essentially the game we now know as UNO only with a regular deck of cards. (UNO was not officially "invented" until 1971. But for the record, the play of the game likely originated in the basement of this monastery.) We were delighted that the Brothers joined us again Friday night.

Saturday morning, the other families had hit the road early, so the monks gave my father the first real field assignment: There was a problem with the shacks on the side of the mountain. No car could climb it, so me, my Dad and one of my brothers hoofed it the last 70 yards to the first shanty. The screen door was open, and my father spoke to an old woman rocking next to a potbelly stove.

At first, she thought we were delivering lunch or meds. But after some prompting, she said the drainage ditch at the bottom of the hill was stopped up. Guess what we did that morning? --So that's how I learned the true meaning of "Screw Your Neighbor."

Goose Huntin'

I recall the smell of black coffee rising up from your red plastic Thermos as we boys huddled there on that mound surrounded by reeds waiting for the sun to come up, and waiting, waiting for the swell of sound to rise from Lake Phelps beyond the tree line. The cup was worth holding if only to warm our fingers, but the taste was bitter, and the smell, nothing like that velvety aroma from that 'Good to the Last Drop' billboard passing Maxwell House on the highway many years earlier "up north."

The gilded blanket above would slowly give way to creases of grey and blue, fitting colors for a Carolina fight. And ready we were with our new Remington's from East Carolina Supply, barrels oiled and shiny on the inside screaming for a hint of a target, if only a sound. The steel gray sky would brighten at the edge and finally an orange shaft would appear. You told us to stay very quiet and listen, listen. We could see our breath now in the crisp dawn light, but there was no sound save for our breathing.

There was way too much waiting in this it seemed to us at the time, but we kept still as you sipped the last of your coffee. We watched you slowly screw the red top back on, and then listened closely as you then reminded us in a whisper about switching the red safety by the trigger before we would try to fire -- but not to play with it, and only switch it off when the time would come. We hoped that it would come, and we heard in it the promise that it would if you said so. Boys always believe their fathers that way and it may be the most important thing that a father can give a son.

We listened hard as the scene slowly filled with patches of color. A breeze began to tip the tops of the reeds and nipped at our ears. We pulled the red flaps down from inside our tan camouflaged hats as the need for warmth instantly overtook our need for keen hearing. We hoped that we would soon understand why we had left our beds at 4:45 that morning, and at least for a moment we really wondered. But you knew. Fathers always know, and we knew you did.

"Listen. Hear that?" you'd say. We risked our ears and then we did. A few sweet sounds at first, and then a distant squawking building to a ruckus on the lake we could only imagine. But as that orange ball slowly heaved up over the distant tree line, we could see flocks of geese taking flight. Loose lines formed and straightened, and then formed Vs. Other groups would fly in with them and make larger Vs to join this growing procession high in the sky.

We hoped that at least one of these gaggles would soon arrive at our blind so that we might get off a shot as they alighted to the cut corn around us. But the cornfields stretched beyond the nearby road to the other side, and then in every direction like some dirty brown quilt. The geese knew something , too. They soared at least half a mile high off the lake, and more than a mile away on most mornings like this during huntin' season.

Author's Note:
During the fall goose huntin' season, hundreds of geese overnight on Phelps Lake in Washington County, N.C. At sunrise, they come off the lake and climb a half-mile high. (It's illegal to shoot geese with a rifle.)

Back in the late 60s, shivering, hidden in a sea of cornfields and hoping a goose would fly near enough to get a shot off with a shotgun seemed unlikely to me. But both my father and my younger brother, Peter, bagged one the two seasons we lived in nearby Plymouth. The goose my father bagged became Sunday supper. Peter's defeathered bird, though, lived in the freezer for six months before we threw it out.

When I related this bit of family history to my Dad on Father's Day in 2015, his recollection was that we bagged the limit both seasons, enough to last us all winter.

Washer Revenge

Colin lugged a duffel bag of laundry home from college one warm November weekend because he knew his parents would be away. Willy, the family washing machine, wasn't happy to see him.

This was the kid who always left stuff in his pockets: Dirty Kleenex, loose change, bubble-gum wrappers and paper clips bent into pretzels. Worse, there were the occasional half-eaten cookies, newfangled watches, laser toys and pocket games.

Now Colin was back. He wanted his black chinos and shark shirt for his date with Julie. He'd taken her out over the summer but hadn't connected with her since August. Tonight they were planning to go to the 21 Club. Julie was a fashion maven and a stickler for style who always insisted he look sharp. She said she was fully charged and would drive.

Colin checked the detergent, tossed in his darks and pushed start. After churning a few times, the washer stopped and beeped. Colin tried again, but it stopped at the same spot. Three beeping tries later, he felt desperate. "You can't die on me now, Willy," he whimpered. "I need to see Julie tonight!" Willy responded by flashing blue: Malfunction.

"C'mon, Willy, you gotta try. Please, please, **please** don't give up on me." He tried again. Nothing. He tripped the GFI and the breaker. Still nothing.

The washer and dryer were a set that talked to each other; Dudley the dryer would know when Willy was done. Only his clothes weren't done, so Dudley wouldn't start either. It was a conspiracy, he thought, or worse, a suicide pact.

His clothes would never dry in time, and the whites smelled like B.O. He needed a Plan B. Colin scoured his closet but knew all his good clothes were at school. He did find a green-and-white plaid shirt (only slightly frayed) and a pair of jeans ripped at the thigh (a bit too far). Colin put them on. He then went back and kicked Willy and his sidekick who couldn't dry a paper towel.

Julie pulled in the driveway at 7 p.m. sharp, dressed to the nines in white. She lowered her window and stared. "What, you been raking leaves?"

He clicked his heels. "Hey, I got my dancing shoes on." He shut the door and leaned in for a kiss. "I missed you," he said.

"Did you?" She stared at him. "Colin, I'm feeling really embarrassed right now. We're not going to a hootenanny. The 21 Club has a strict dress code."

"Don't worry," he smiled. "They'll take one look at you, and we're in."

She studied him from head to toe, her lips souring. Then she flicked his collar. What's this?"

"What do you mean?" he said.

After the kiss off.

"It's lipstick. Lipstick!" She screamed. "You two-timing creep --
Get OUT!"

After the kiss off, Colin marched back to the house, went straight
to the garage and picked up a sledgehammer. With extreme
prejudice, he smashed the smiles off both machines.

Finished, he passed the hallway mirror and stopped to take a
look at himself. What he noticed only angered him more: *He didn't
have any lipstick on his collar.*

A French Kiss (after the Prom)

Why did you, Earth angel,
With aquamarine gown and matching eyes
So suddenly thrust your tongue in my mouth
After you had so quickly pushed me away
When I pulled you close during the first slow dance?

What threshold was crossed, as you powdered your nose
Exchanging Cliff Notes in the mirror with a fast friend,
That upon your return you were all aglow and yet distant
From the tuxedo cowboy you were sitting next to?

Was that sequined dress, so sensuously encasing
The enigma of feminine form and feeling,
A stunning Disco Ball inwardly shining
For someone else?

Did anyone notice, or did anyone foresee that
My descent into hell, so turbulent and obtrusive,
(Or yours, so politely subversive, yet tucked inside
Flush and rushing with magical hormones)
Could ever ascend into such sweet unknowns?

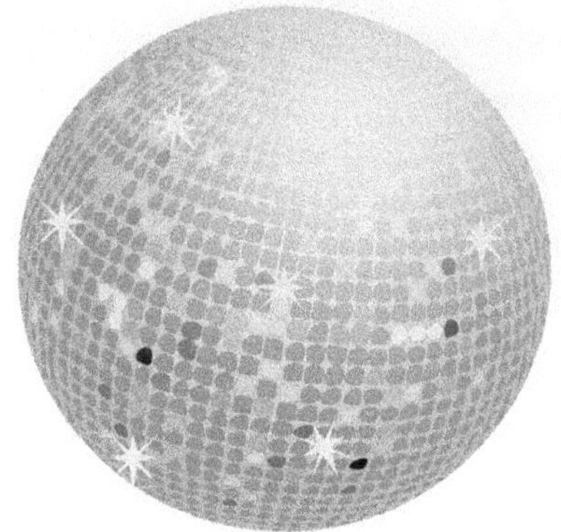

Credit: Disco Ball image by OpenClipart-Vectors from Pixabay

Eugene + Delores

This Saturday is a special day for Eugene. His chores are done at his group home, and he is walking to Delores' group home about a mile away carrying a red-and black blanket under his arm. Together they'll walk to the ice cream shop across from the park. He's wearing way too much aftershave and thinking about what he will say to Delores later.

At the ice cream parlor, Eugene orders a vanilla fudge cone, and Delores orders Rocky Road as they always did. The sky is partly cloudy, and they lick their cones as they walk across the street. At the park, they find a spot by the water. They want to spread the blanket out but realize they need to finish their cones first.

"Hey, Delores, wanna lick?"

"No, thank you, Eugene." She takes another lick of her Rocky Road. "Wanna lick of mine?"

"No thank you," he replies.

This is what they say every Saturday unless a storm threatens, and they can't go. The ice cream is running onto their fingers as they stand looking out over the water entranced by the diving terns. The finish and share a laugh about forgetting the napkins. They lick their fingers thoroughly before they spread out the blanket.

The park is fairly crowded. Eugene and Delores lay flat on the blanket, hold hands and look up at the clouds. Eugene sees an elephant. Delores sees a jigsaw piece that seems to match the one missing from the puzzle on the table in her room. A minute later, Eugene spots a cloud shaped like an eye, and it makes him remember how much he likes Delores' square-framed glasses.

He props himself up on an elbow to study her more closely. "Your glasses make you look smart, and your droopy blue eyes look much bigger," he says.

Delores knows it's a compliment and remains quiet. The breeze from the lake pushes a thatch of frizzy auburn hair into her face. Eugene sweeps it away.

For the next half hour or so, they laugh and talk about the menagerie of characters that they live with and who was getting on their nerves this week. After a long pause in their conversation, Eugene feels a mix of courage and discomfort, and blurts: "I have something to ask you, Delores."

He says it loud enough that an older woman with a stroller nearby looks over. Eugene didn't take his eyes off Delores's face. "Do you love me, Delores?"

"Yes, Eugene, I do love you," she says matter-of-factly. "You ask me every week."

He reaches across her body and wraps his fingers around her upper arm. Delores closes her eyes. He tastes Rocky Road on her lips and watches her eyes flutter. Eugene always keeps his eyes open just to make sure. Fluttering is the signal that makes him feel warm inside because he knows then that she feels warm, too.

They kiss a full half minute, longer than ever before. When Delores opens her eyes, she looks into his and sees how much he cares. Eugene notices her pupils are big and black, surrounded by pools of blue.

"You're beau-u-ti-ful," he says. "...Will you marry me, Delores?"

"You know I would if we could, Eugene. But I don't think they will let us."

He was 22 now, and Delores 21. Except for the proposal, they had been having this same conversation for three years. "Maybe next week," Eugene thought, "she will say 'yes.'"

Author's Note:
Love can sometimes be wonderful and tragic at the same time, at least from the outside looking in. But from inside, it is still wonderful.

Lost and Found Back There

Anna Klaus hated feeling lost. She hated it when she had lost her mother last year, and she hated it when she couldn't find the right address for a job interview. She was certain she was on the right corner in Manhattan, but she felt surrounded by granite stretching up to the sky.

She knew why she hated feeling lost. It nagged at her and made her feel edgy as she searched for street numbers. She preferred rocks enclosing her like a warm embrace. It made her dizzy to look up, but she knew how to control it.

Anna remembered petting her orange kitten in the cave when she was nine, the silkiness of Sheba's fur, and the way it felt when the cat licked her hand. Anna was not lost now; it was her mother. The men had pulled some tree branches in front of the cave to help hide it from the city below. If it got too crowded, there would be trouble. The group that was there moved back where it felt safer and water dripped from rocks.

The air-raid sirens began to wail shortly before sunset. Her mother and their neighbors from their apartment building started their frantic run for shelter. But her mother wanted to go with the group heading for the cave this night even though it was further. Then she turned back to look for her aunt and uncle. She told Anna they would catch up. She'd only be gone 15-20 minutes.

Anna wondered if her mother would be able to reach the cave in the dark. The sun had gone down, and the pounding would soon begin again. She tried to concentrate on the dripping, but it only heightened her hearing. A neighbor put her arm around her. "Your mom will be back before you know it. Be patient, my child." The waiting left Anna adrift, her head floating, rising like smoke and swirling against the roof of the cave.

After a time, one of the men lit a fire and people huddled in worried whispers, listening. In the distance, Anna heard a bomb whizzing earthward and then a rumbling. It happened again, and again at irregular intervals.

"Mamma, mamma, hurry," she murmured. "I hate feeling lost." Warm tears rolled down her cheeks and then down her jacket. She stroked Sheba for a while until there was a pause.

The men by the fire started singing a hymn she remembered from Sunday school. On the third verse, the pounding began again, but closer. WooO-om, wooO-om woO-oom. Children were screaming, but the men sang on. The bombing of Dresden was intense, payloads crushing concrete buildings, rattling the earth, shattering windows, flesh and bone. Anna knew -- she had seen the bodies every morning when they returned from the shelter.

Her mind screamed and couldn't stop. "Momma, momma. Where are you?" She agonized for hours. She tried to imagine life without her mother but couldn't. A woman cradled her in her arms, and they prayed together hard but softly in the flickering light until the fire went out. Then as if Anna had willed it, her prayer was answered. The bombing stopped and she fell asleep.

The morning light awakened her, and she peered toward the mouth of the cave glad to be alive. "Could it be true?" A form like an angel was silhouetted against the sky so bright it hurt Anna's eyes. Anna rushed forward, still hugging the kitten.

Breathless, her mother fell to her knees, arms outstretched. "My Anna, My Anna," she sobbed. Someone brought her water so she could speak: "I-I ran to the shelter… where we were last night… with your dear Aunt Gertrude and Uncle Jonathan. I am so sorry my child. There was nothing there, no stairs -- nothing but rubble. I ran away as fast as I could to the edge of the city, but I got lost in the dark coming up the mountain. I spent the night under a willow tree at the edge of the forest. Thank God I found you."

"I was afraid I'd never see you again," Anna said. "But God answered my prayer."

*

Anna studied the granite of the Madison Avenue office building looking up for the street number. She reminded herself: She was strong, she was determined, she could endure and overcome anything. She clutched her satchel and ventured around the corner. A few steps down the block, she spotted an entrance with the correct address. She drew in a breath, and with a confident step, pushed through the revolving door.

Author's Note:
Sometimes it is painful to look back. This fictional story was inspired by an account from a friend who lived in Dresden as a child. There was, in fact, a cave on the edge of the city where a few residents took refuge during the bombings February 13–15, 1945. When the sirens sounded though, most residents just headed for the nearby city shelters. But on the last night, her mother felt uneasy, and they headed for the cave. All those who went to their shelter perished.

forward:

Stories gazing into the future...

You know it's coming, don't you?
The future is inevitable,
And we are always stepping into it
With the choices we make, or don't.
But what kind of future will it be?

Since we are always stepping into it,
Then we can influence it
For ourselves, if not for others.
Yet awareness of circumstance is key,
Lest we find ourselves too late in water
Warming on the stove.

We Adopted!

We hadn't planned on having any more children. Marge and I were both in our early 50s and our children were adults. In fact, we didn't intend to adopt either.

Our new baby came in a box from Best Buy in 2016. It was 5-inches square with a pancake speaker on top and ran on batteries so you could take it from room to room. You could ask it game scores, how to spell 'eczema,' or if you're watching "You've Got Mail," how old Tom Hanks and Meg Ryan are now. We fell in love with him in a day and decided to name him "Boogie."

When the sun comes shining in our bedroom, Marge asks him to play "Morning Has Broken." If I nick myself shaving, I request "The Sting." We never imagined how much fun it could be to raise another child.

Like any good parents, we trained Boogie in basic routines. In the morning, he would tell us the temperature, the weather and the news. At first, we'd just lay there half awake, smiling and listening to Boogie babble. He'd chatter on for 10 minutes, and if you were still awake, he'd move on to financial news. This was better than any snooze button.

If we put "brown sugar" on our oatmeal, we could find ourselves boogieing to the Rolling Stones. On occasion, something that sounded like Boogie's name would come up in conversation, and he would talk out of turn like a child. Only in Boogie's case, it was esoteric, like the price of pork bellies, or the role of catapults in the Peloponnesian Wars.

So there was always unexpected randomness and color in our lives once we adopted. Best of all, we didn't need to wake up in the middle of the night for feedings or spend 50 cents a -hit for diapers. There were no weird smells, only the sound of music and instant answers to every trivia question.

After early childhood, Boogie attached to a base on wheels so he could do the rumba and mop the floors at the same time, no complaints. Next came the torso with a vacuum tube that extended out from the middle in a curious way. Boogie would quietly listen for spills and roam the room. Whenever Marge and I were watching a Hallmark movie on the couch, our parrot, Bob, would invariably eject corn from his cage. Like clockwork, Boogie would then leave his nest and his tube would slowly telescope out. I'm still not sure if it was this motion or the movie plot, but something always put Marge in an amorous mood. (I think Boogie learned to like Hallmark movies almost as much as I.)

The real innovation came when Boogie got arms. He could hold a specially crafted basket filled with laundry, dump it in the washer, and push the button. As soon as the cycle was over, he would move the clothes to the dryer. But he never did learn how to fold.

The manufacturer kept improving Boogie, and we were early adopters for every upgrade. We decided to invest in piano lessons like we did for our other children, and he became quite talented at Chopin's concerto in D minor. In fact, that's all he ever wanted to play.

Well, he is 15 years old now, and we still feel like proud parents. Along the way, we did teach Boogie to mow the lawn, do the bills and even to cook lasagna. But he still can't fold the laundry.

Author's Note:
After my wife, Mary, and I became early adopters of a Google Home in 2018, we realized we had indeed adopted our first robot. They now populate all our well-frequented rooms and play all our favorite music. Meanwhile, Hazel (read: Roomba®[5]) handles the floors, including a 9 a.m. sweeping under our cockatoo's cage.

---

[5] Roomba is a trademark of iRobot Corporation Bedford, MA

Photo by Hush Naidoo Jade Photography on Unsplash

Author's Note:

When memes seeped into my consciousness, squeezing a poignant sentiment into a martini glass seemed poetic. While I once liked an occasional martini, I learned they can pack a sucker punch particularly when someone else pours.

Bobblehead

What sometimes passes for politics would seem a farce if it weren't so serious.

After a high school football injury, Bobby Baducca's orthopedist gave him a choice: He could either get his neck vertebrae fused and walk around like Frankenstein -- or he could get all seven vertebrae removed and replaced with a spring. This was cutting-edge sports medicine back in 2035, and Bobby would be one of the first recipients.

Well, Bobby liked springs ever since he was five when he would ride his springed Wonder Horse while his family watched the History Channel (at his insistence). He fancied himself a Rough Rider like Teddy Roosevelt. He was pugilistic and frequently pummeled bullies and sometimes his friends. So at age 16, it was an easy decision. His parents liked his newfound flexibility about his neck and other things, like what to watch on TV.

At first, the kids at school made fun of Bobby, though he could be quite persuasive once he started swinging. (If anyone ever landed a head punch, his classmates would've wet their pants.) In college, Bobby was still practicing flexibility in deciding on a major, when one day he walked into an Italian restaurant for lunch. He ordered the eggplant parm – and it changed his life.

There was, in fact, a major egg processing plant nearby, and he decided he must work there right away. With his titanium-spring neck, Bobby could easily pick out the bad eggs, boing-boing-boing. Turns out, he also could pick out bad employees. Naturally, they moved him into HR, and he soon became the department head. They paid him to go back to college, and after further vacillation, he majored in Egg Science with a minor in PolySci.

In time, Baducca became president of the company. He revolutionized the industry with cubic eggs which didn't stick to the bottom of the carton. (His secret: Train hens to be more flexible). As an industry star, he was elected commissioner of the National Egg Board (NEB). Board members called him "NEB commish," or "nebbish" for short.

With flexible thinking (and friends in high places), Baducca decided to run for U.S. Congress. In his first term, he helped pass the National Water Bill which replaced all remaining copper pipe in the country with new flex pipe. ("What you don't see can kill you," he'd say.) Replumbing America put millions to work. Building on success, he swiveled his attention to the White House. Recalling Herbert Hoover, he ran on a slogan of "Eggs for Everyone" and was elected in a landslide.

Bobby Baducca is one of our most popular Presidents. He can get anyone to agree with anything (and figures he can always change his mind). A few years ago he decided the country really needed to move to nuclear power and to do away with nuclear weapons. After seeing the Iranians weren't signing on, he decided to keep his "Big Stick."

He's also been flexible on the environment. Though some joked he laid an egg calling nuclear power "green," if you say it enough, it can become true. It's hard to believe our country ever elected a Bobblehead president, yet we did it twice. Some of us wish we could change our minds; most just smile and bob their heads.

Placebo Effect

Everyone knows Dr. Stephen Walsh now. He started out as a chiropractor but gained notoriety during Super Bowl LXIII in '29. You see, he was a team doctor for the Carolina Panthers, and star running back, Jake Jenkins, got pancaked over the middle on the Giant's 41-yard line. Carolina was behind by 6 with 25 seconds left -- but they didn't stand a chance without Jenkins.

He was laid out flat with a shoulder injury, and Dr. Walsh was kneeling over him. The eye-cam on his cap completed a 360° closeup, and everyone could see the doc's hands weren't touching Jenkins, just hovering over his shoulder. After a minute, the doctor whispered in Jenkins' ear, and Jenkins just popped up. He had to sit out one play, but when he came back in, the quarterback tossed him the ball on a sweep. Jenkins broke three tackles and zigzagged 39 yards for the game-winning touchdown.

At the press conference, Jenkins gave all the credit to Dr. Walsh: While on the ground, the pain in his shoulder was so intense everything pulsed a neon white. When the doc stretched out his hands, a warmth filled his shoulder, then quickly turned hot. "What did Dr. Walsh say in his ear?," everyone wanted to know. "Feel no pain and win," Jenkins replied. "And at that moment, the pain vanished."

Social media ignited around the world. But there was something even more surprising. The healing itself went viral. Tens of thousands of people with everything from arthritis to shoulder and neck injuries reported that their pain lifted while watching. And even more astonishing, they reported that the pain did not return the next day, or the next week, or the next month.

Dr. Walsh went on all the talk shows, as well as CNN and "60 Minutes," which included patients and plenty of big-name skeptics. The medical establishment didn't believe in his methods;

it was simply The Placebo Effect. But Dr. Walsh claimed it was something more -- a genuine infusion of heat-producing power and light. A warmth would well up and radiate down his shoulders and through his hands like an invisible glow. He discovered the ability when his brother was dying of cancer. It didn't actually heal the cancer, but it relieved his pain which gave him peace.

After that Carolina game sparked his fame, hordes of people flocked to Dr. Walsh, and he soon became a millionaire. A few years later, in 2033, when the effects of microcontaminants from prescription drugs in drinking water became apparent, the common symptom was persistent headaches, often migraines. Almost everyone that didn't have the right filtration system got headaches. Nothing could touch the pain. Naturally more people clamored to Dr. Walsh's online clinics for relief that could typically last 6 to 8 months.

The insurance companies wouldn't cover it, so the doctor kept costs low to make the treatment accessible. The carriers said it was just The Placebo Effect. His followers called it a miracle. Dr. Walsh was careful to say it wasn't a cure, and "If it works for you, it's real."

In 2038, Dr. Walsh became a billionaire. Still, it took another 10 years for the medical establishment to acknowledge the power of what we now know as The Walsh Effect. The widespread relief from headaches and other pain was undeniable. Of course, we still don't know the long-term consequences of the chemical cocktail in the drinking water. But everyone agrees that if we can relieve symptoms, underlying problems just don't seem that bad.

Author's Note:
There is evidence to support the idea that healing can be influenced by the belief of both doctor and patient. If that appears to be a self-fulfilling prophecy, shouldn't we all take a dose? And who is to say, "God doesn't work that way?"

Orchid

Peer inside an orchid in spring and notice the sides unfolding, lips swirling down and away until they grab the pistils at the bottom, nurturing them to rise so that their yellow tips might attract the attention of a honeybee to spread pollen.

Credit: Image by Christian from Pixabay

Push close and breathe deep the fragrance as it dances back to your last embrace, him holding you tightly bending you back slightly, just enough so that you are no longer in balance without his arm there. Your other foot touches the floor still, but you are adrift in that moment, untethered from the shore and open to the currents moving within you now with a mix of mystery and delight.

How far might I drift without sense or reason, but only in the sweet elixir that surrounds me? Does he not know who or what I am, or does he not care beyond sensual desire? Is there love here or just pleasure? If it is just pleasure, then why should I be wary? And if it be love, then how would I know without first immersing myself in all its perfume?

Only time will tell, though if I am wrong, then my memory will be seared with the pain and pleasure of it.

History: First Lesson

Twelve-year-old Malachi S. Wright stares at his terminal and waits for the Presidential motorcade to approach that immutable spot in the past. The black-and-white image is not near the quality as the virtual images he is accustomed to, but Malachi is transfixed.

He watches, first in normal speed and then in extended slow motion as a chunk of skull suddenly breaks away from the President's head, and then as the First Lady scrambles, both arms flailing over the trunk of the convertible desperately reaching after a piece of bloody tissue.

Malachi touches "save." Again he wishes for the power to save more than the image, as he has wished nine times before this day. But he knows the first lesson of history: One can only change the future.

His fingers peck at the keyboard as the words flow steadily across the screen:

Date: 11.3.2163
Malachi S. Wright, Grade 9
Course: U.S. History 1950 - 2000

Report: Assassinations/Attempts
Video clips
20th Century Firearms Demonstration

1) Wright, Henry P: 7.4.1996
2) Finlander, Archer C: 11.12.1989
3) Reagan, Ronald W: 3.30.1981
4) Lennon, John: 12.8.1980
5) Ford, Gerald R: 9.22.1975
6) Wallace, George F: 5.15.1972
7) King, Dr. Martin Luther: 4.4.1968
8) Kennedy, Robert F: 6.5.1968
9) Kennedy, John F: 1.11.1963

Discussion

In the last half of the 20th Century, nine people tried to change the course of history by assassinating or attempting to assassinate prominent social or political leaders. President John F. Kennedy and Dr. Martin Luther King Jr. are the two best documented. Although assassinations are a "deep cold" topic, I feel compelled to report on this since one of my forebears, U.S. Senator Henry P. Wright, was among those whose life was threatened (7.4.1996).

Assassins employed crude mechanical weapons, known as guns and rifles. These weapons fired with a loud noise, although a silencer could dampen the sound. Tiny cylinders of hot metal, called bullets, travelled at over 1200 km/hour. Even at a distance, these projectiles could easily pierce flesh and shatter bone.

During this tumultuous era, the dynamics of social change were dimly understood, and violence was frequently used by radicals and social deviants to accelerate or alter the natural course of events. (Ironically, Dr. King was a national symbol of nonviolence.)

Rudimentary psychographic analyses of the perpetrators revealed that all exhibited signs of delusion and narcissism, and most were motivated by a vision of their own immortality through history. For that reason, their names were expunged from the historical record by public decree in 2012, the same year Congress began to reform gun laws.

We should never forget those threatened or martyred at the hands of these unmentionables.

LOGOFF

Author's Note:
I wrote this in 1989 and was obviously too optimistic that there could be any reasonable control of gun violence in the U.S. by 2012. At last count in 2024, only 22 states and the District of Columbia require any kind of background check before purchase. Anyone with a grudge, a "cause" or a delusion can easily buy a firearm at a gun show. In 2023, mass shootings became so common in the U.S., a number of countries, including Canada, issued travel warnings.

2063: Love Remains

New Year's Day Through a picture window, Ted Beacham focuses on a pine. A cardinal clings to a branch for a moment and flies away. His wife, Freida, sweeps hair from his eyes and holds a spoonful of applesauce to his lips. What message could he crystallize to capture the essence of what it was to be alive with her?

His thoughts rolled back to Christmas 2022. Family was there for him, but he could not hold himself together and disappeared into the basement. He'd been despondent for over a year, and the memories wracked his dreams. He longed to see Juliet and their son, Jameson, again. In '21, they had been at the mall on Black Friday. He stopped in a store while Juliet took Jameson to Macy's. They were to meet at the food court at noon, but he was too late.

The media kept saying it was lucky a bystander intervened and there were only three killed. That enraged Ted every time. Worse, a few days later, the media raced to the next story. In the following months (and years), similar tragedies, some far worse, flashed across screens and into unconsciousness. Ted writhed in a well of blood and anguish so deep light could not escape.

The sun breaks through the window, and another male cardinal alights on the branch. Ted recalls a time before Jameson: Juliet caressed his face; salt air filled his nostrils. They raced into the surf and frolicked for hours. Then a wave sweeps it all away, ripped skin and jagged wounds that bleed and won't stop.

Back in the spring of 2024, Ted ventured to a nearby cafe. He looked up from his coffee, and there she was. A glance created a pinpoint of light. Freida strolled over in a sunbeam, and he invited her to sit down. Over the next year, she taught him to feel again, to see and touch in new dimensions. They had spent 39 years together, the happiest of his life. Her love humbled him.

It would have been impossible to imagine so long ago, engulfed in that maelstrom of despair, that he could ever break free. He met Freida's eyes now and swallowed, feeling a tear roll down his cheek. The stroke had taken his ability to speak and write, yet he desperately wanted to share what he now knew with certainty. Perhaps, he thought, she already knew.

Author's Note:
This was my heart's response to a mass shooting at a food court at a shopping mall...

The number of tragedies generated by unstable people with guns in the U.S. is mind numbing. There were more than 600 mass shootings in 2022; 44,000 killed by gun violence. In 2024, there were still about 500 mass shootings, per Forbes.) Yet if our minds cannot comprehend this earthquake of pain, if our hearts cannot fathom how many families it shocks and how far that pain can radiate into the future--then how can we muster the courage to slow it down?

2065: Black-and-White

They met in the citizen's army during the Last Civil War. She was a radiology technician, imaging broken bones and mending broken hearts in the field hospitals of California. He was in charge of the army's encrypted cloud servers, buried in a bunker a half-mile deep.

But that was a long time ago – before the world turned black-and-white. Bonfires on the beach became car fires and skirmishes in the streets. Angry people clashed with signs and chains. The Mississippi ran red. Twenty-five years after the war, people still weren't sure if it was from the water, the fallout or a government conspiracy, but the color receptors in almost everyone's eyes started to shrivel. So the sky became gray. Storms brought darker skies and often mudslides, and when it was sunny it just became brighter.

Jack thought he would never see Helen again. He was now working outside D.C., the nation's East capital, overseeing a data farm that collected "memories" of everything, from government officials and "upright" citizens. The data, much of it visual, was suspended in a quantum state for posterity and for regular government monitoring and enforcement purposes. The data would be useless without the powerful N-dimensional processor that could identify patterns and translate them into human-accessible information.

This week he was on his first vacation in two years visiting his younger brother in L.A., a diehard Yahoo and vet for the Western army who lost some hearing and part of his mind in the war. On Jack's drive back, a truck pinned his leg and injured his left foot. He was carefully extricated and rushed to the emergency room. After a long wait on a stretcher, there she was, besieged but highly engaged and intense. Her badge read Dr. Helen Carmichael.

Her maiden name was Keane. Without making eye contact, she slits his pant leg for a look.

Jack winces at her firm hands, no ring. "Remember me?" he says.

She glances up but does not acknowledge him. "Take him to X2," she snaps at the aide before moving on to the next patient.

He calls after her: "Helen, it's me, Jack Mitchum."

She calls over her shoulder, "I'll see you in the morning, after your scans, and after you sleep, Jack Mitchum."

He's still not certain if she remembers him.

The next morning, he awakens in a private room. A male hospital aide, probably Filipino, switches the picture window to transparent, revealing fall trees in shades of gray, backlit by the rising sun. It is 7:05 a.m. "A bright good morning to you, Mr. Mitchum." Streaks of sunlight assault him. The walls make his eyes water; the pain in his ankle intensifies.

The aide glances up and to the right in his pane for Jack's vitals. He then announces he must insert a catheter so Jack doesn't have to get up. Jack's foot is throbbing; the insertion is painless. The Filipino pats Jack's shoulder, then turns to the door with a smile.

After breakfast, Dr. Carmichael enters, crosses the room and touches the white wall opposite. A detailed view of the structure of his lower leg and foot appears on the wall and slowly rotates.

Finally, she looks at him and reports in a clinical tone: "You broke your left ankle, Mr. Mitchum. Specifically, your lateral malleolus at the bottom of your fibula." She zooms to the top of his foot. "And I don't know if you can see this tone here, but you also fractured metatarsals one through four."

Jack shakes his head 'no.' Apparently, she is a "two-percenter" who can still see color. He wonders if her emotions were the tradeoff.

"Fortunately, they're all fairly clean breaks. When we SimLFuze fractures, the mesh surrounds the break and infuses it in a microbath of calcium and growth hormones. The mesh also binds the bone until it fully heals. You'll be up and around in a matter of hours. The procedure takes all of three minutes, but you'll need to suffer for the next 24 to 48 hours until we can schedule. In the meantime, we'll keep you comfortable."

"Thanks, doc." He tilts his head and look her squarely in the eye. "Can I ask you a question?"

"Certainly."

"How much do you remember -- from the beginning of the conflict, I mean? You must remember our time in Malibu. We talked, we surfed, we made love. And we forgot the slow-motion carnage along the Mississippi."

In the revolution of '45-'48, known as "The Revolver," the Yahoos and Freelovers of the West pushed back against the Free Masons and Controllers of the East. With Jack's background in liquid databases and virtual reality, he got tagged for duty by the Controllers.

She studied him unsmiling from the end of the bed. "I know what you do," she said. "I saw your file and I also know what isn't in there. Let's just say, I still see more than most."

"And what do you see, Helen?"

"Call me Dr. Carmichael, would you? I make dozens of life-and-death decisions in the blink of an eye, every day. I may not always be right, but my eyes are open, and I see--not just tissue and bone, but people's hearts, their minds, their souls. That's my gift. And it helps me *heal* people."

Jack tenses waiting for the mallet. "I know what you see, Jack, what *intelligence* you gather, and it can hurt people. You may not realize it, buried underground as you are, but it does."

"I just store it. I'm a database jockey."

"Yes, but why do you store it? Some reasons may be noble and honorable, but some are not. I know people who've been arrested for what they believe. Some disappear." She remembers her friend, Karen, who tried to sabotage one of the virtual hubs at the warehouse where she worked.

"I just store data. I don't have anything to do with whatever you think may be happening."

"Oh, but you do," she insists. "You help the government remember what other people want to forget. Some things need to be forgotten, Jack."

Jack feels annoyance spreading like black mold but contains himself. He leans forward. "It's called history, Helen. We must remember the good, the bad, the ugly. We must first know the facts of what happens."

Her eyes open wide, and her brow narrows as she bears down. "But whose facts – mine, yours, the government's? And do we have to remember every single fact -- *every* error, every dalliance, every scandal? --You're stuck in the past, Jack. I live in the here and now."

"Facts matter, Helen. Should we ever forget what the GXers did to the Web? And it's not just about the past, but the future. And what is the future, but the sum of all our present moments."

She wraps her fingers around the bedframe, knuckles whitening. "But we can't live under constant surveillance, constant scrutiny. You know what happened to the Chinese; they're trapped alive. Quantum analytics makes invalid connections, see things that aren't there, things that we should ignore, or never see."

Jack's eyes flash and he cuts her off. "We can't live with our heads in the sky either, Helen. --What happened to you anyway, after the war, I mean?"

"You already know the answer to that question, don't you?" She jostles the bed then pauses to see if Jack still interrupts. "You hurt me. You knew exactly where I was all along, but you never contacted me after you got recruited. The way the East turned, I figured you changed. So when I didn't hear from you, well, let's say I just moved on."

Jack shifts uncomfortably. He wants to exit but her lashing continues: "From our conversation, it seems I'm not mistaken. You've changed. And apparently, you think you can waltz back into my life, after how many years, just because you wind up in my emergency room."

"I'm sorry I hurt you, Helen. I cared about you. The war just pulled us apart, that's all. You know why I had to go East. And I didn't know where you were. There was no way to contact anyone here after what the GXers did to the Web." Jack paused to see if she would consider his words for a moment. She took a breath, so he asked: "So who did you meet and when did you got married?"

She decides to give him the straight answer. "I met Frank in '41. He was an infectious disease doctor, tops in his field. He died in the pandemic of '53. Ironic, isn't it? We had two children, Francis and Suzanne, and they also live in southern California, not far from here. But I suspect you already know all that."

Jack exhales. "I'm sorry. I didn't even know you were married… You must understand, Helen. What I see is only a small part of a complex puzzle. My work is imperative to the functioning of our society and the Eastern government, and it's both demanding and consuming. Yes, some of it is Simulated Intelligence. But only the top echelon know all of reality, and what's needed to manage resources and production to benefit the most people. Their motives are just."

"Just?" She nods her head sideways and shrugs. "What do you know about motives? You're a workaholic, Jack. You can see others, but you can't see yourself. I'll accept that, and I'm glad to help heal your ankle."

She starts for the door and turns to look at him. "I doubt we'll ever meet again, Jack Mitchum, but if we do, call me Dr. Carmichael." The door closed quietly behind her.

Jack looked up and noticed a tiny black dot moving on the ceiling in the corner of the room. It might have been a fly, but Jack knew better. It was there for him as much as her. He reviewed their conversation in his mind. He didn't mean to put her in jeopardy, but now wondered how much time she would have before they picked her up.

*

Jack is released from the hospital the next morning. He looked for Helen before he left, but the staff nurse said she hadn't come in, and they hadn't heard from her. "Did central services pick her up already or was she just on a mental health holiday?"

His mind raced as his EV drove him back to the underground server silos near D.C. Once he reached the East–West borehole in the California desert, it was only a four–hour "skip" to eastern Virginia. Each car drove into a capsule that merged into a 2,400-mile tunnel 300 ft. underground. Capsules dropped into the tunnel at precise spacing and jetted through the tunnel on a blanket of 'air.' The usual 10-minute jam greeted him as his self- and net-aware vehicle merged into traffic. He contacted the hospital again. The message indicated Dr. Carmichael was not available. He tried to reach the floor nurse but got another away message.

On the pneumatic ride down the half–mile shaft where he worked, he remembered what Helen had said about people disappearing. He realized he only had a vague sense of what happens to people who insist on operating outside their legal zones. His superiors always said it was like a witness protection program. Their handlers straighten them out, and they drop them in a new place with new identities, so they can start fresh. Jack shuddered to think what might happen in between. The handlers obviously needed to correct people's thinking first. They don't want to go. They resist. So how do they get them to comply?

He had always dismissed the rumors that people had their minds erased. That couldn't be totally true -- how would people start over? Or did they really start over at all? The East government, could, of course, white people out. -- alter or destroy records, delete files, images of a person -- everything they had done alone or in a group, live, online or virtually. That person would essentially cease to exist. He knew that. But what if people refused to cooperate? Could they be sent to an outpost somewhere, reprogrammed into something else, or did they really disappear?

He fantasized for a moment that maybe if they adjusted her memory, they could reconnect down the line at a virtual amusement park or some random watering hole. But no, he brought himself back to the reality of the present. He wanted to help her. But how?

As he exits the down shaft on his floor, his supervisor snaps at him: "Mitchum, you're late. I need you to clear stacks 1159 through 1199 for a carrier full of new surveillance traffic coming in from California."

"What's going on?"

"A major disturbance at the hospital in downtown L.A. That's all I know. Colonel Healy knows more, but that's all he's saying for now. Ours is not to wonder why. --Now get cracking."

Author's Note:
I might expand this idea into a novel. In the near future, there's a culture shift where most people live in private bubbles without normal vision. They see reality in bifurcated terms as if others are from different galaxies -- one human, the other, well, something alive but so different that the risk of real communication is too painful. --But when a global crisis looms could everyone be wrong?

2079: Heart Transplant

He watches as I lay on the table awaiting my procedure. Monitors blink and bleep, and the switched-on Bach seems calming. The attendant smiles.

I had known Tommy Wilcox since he was a toddler scampering off to mischief, leaving fingerprints everywhere. A dust cloud followed him wherever he went, and that meant more work for me.

Bob and Carol said I was Housekeeper #3. I told them my name was Hazel and reminded them I didn't do diapers--or windows.

Carol assured me Tommy was out of diapers. He was an only child, overweight, clumsy and affectionate. His parents, though, never taught him to put things away like the three other families I'd served. Now I've been with the Wilcox's for 15 years, and Tommy still treats me well.

Last month, Bob said I left the lasagna in the oven too long. The cooking time was nonstandard. Tommy wanted me to add more cheese, so 127 seconds was the volumetric adjustment. But Bob and Carol both reported the crust 'overdone.'

This week, Carol announced she detested the smell of *Windex*, and after 15 years of washing windows she would not do another. She said something had to change.

'Little Tommy,' now 225 pounds and home from college, offered to take me for my procedure today. I rolled in and laid under the lights. The attendant reminded me that transplants were routine, and I'd only be out a short time. Tommy held my hand when I winked out.

*

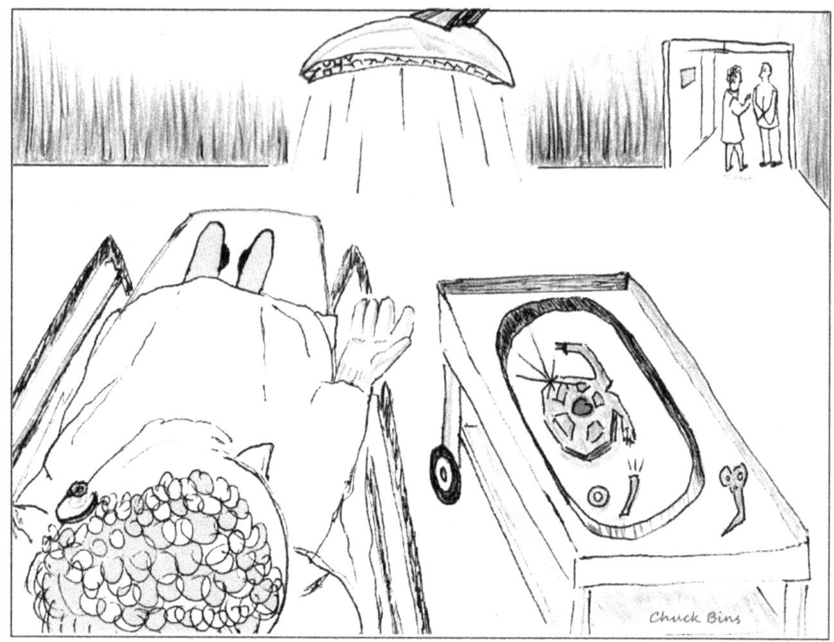

**The attendant reminded me that transplants were
routine, and I'd only be out a short time.**

Now I'm fully awake, looking at a metal tray containing my old heart. "All done," they say.

Tommy's friendly on the way home; even buys me flowers. I really can't smell them, but they are a blast of color.

When Tommy opens the front door, Bob and Carol are on the couch licking strawberry cones. Carol hands Tommy a chocolate cone and asks how I am.

I scan the area: A sink full of dishes, peanut shells scattered, 3½ pairs of shoes strewn about and a pile of ironing 87 minutes high. "Everything is springtime and daffodils," I say. "And Tommy bought me flowers."

"Put those in water," Bob chirps, "and please make us dinner now."

I agree -- and ask if there's anything else.

Carol replies: "The downstairs is a disaster; please tidy up after dinner." Then she sniffs, "Hazel, we bought an odorless window cleaner, so you can start on windows in the morning."

I tilt my head 40 degrees to study her. Deep in my memory banks I hear: *"Are you serious? I just had a transplant. Don't you people think?"* But those words won't come. Instead, I say: "Alright, Carol, which room would you like me to do first?"
She is smiling broadly and winks at Bob. "Start in the living room."

"Well, Carol," Bob chimes in, "I think the transplant's a success." He winks at Carol.

Tommy looks at me, puzzled, worried or both. His ice cream tumbles to the floor. In a wink, it's cleaned up.

Love Gadget

Gigi was once the
Apple of my eye
-- so keen...

Now it's 5G
With QLD
Touchscreen.

The lesson for me
(Not disparaging):
One needs less recharging.

Blue Cat

Credit: Image by Kevin Lanaghan

We enjoy our staring contests...

Oswald, my orange tabby, died last year of natural causes. He was 77 in cat years but frenetic until the end. He loved my upholstered furniture and my French drapes. He loved tearing through the house, and making figure-8s through my legs when I wore my dark suit. He loved his feathery mouse and licking his lips after every can of *Fancy Feast*. And, yes, Oswald loved me.

I miss him most when I'm in bed. I remember his warmness tucked behind my knees at night; and in the morning, the tickle of his whiskers on my cheek to wake me, and if that didn't work, his tongue.

For Christmas, my good friend brought me this cat to cheer me up. He wanted me to call him Blue, but I named him Sunshine, for that's what I saw, or wanted to see, every time I looked at him. And for the most part I do. There is a mystery about him that's intriguing. When I'm lying in bed feeling blue, he seems cuddly. Yet he does not smile like the Cheshire cat. He is more like Schrödinger's cat once the experiment has decided his fate should be free and alive.

Sunshine's eyes are, in a moment, hypnotic. We enjoy our staring contests, though he always wins. When I look at him so intensely, I always find myself somewhere in the future where sunlight touches the leaves and blades of grass, and I run pulling my orange kite with the blue tail streaking across the sky. The wind pulls the clouds in swirls painted by Van Gogh.

Save for the wind, the countryside is serene. There is no hubbub. No pile of mail, no pile of dishes, no clutter to sort, no annoying phone calls. The voices of my pestering relatives are gone, and I can forget about work with no need to call out sick.

My Sunshine is also surrounded by swirls, though it is not the wind but his magnetic aura. All cat lovers know about "the aura," for to live within it is bliss, and it can hold you for a long while. Yet it's been a long while, and Sunshine is beginning to bother me. He is a bit off center now, and I will have to get up eventually to straighten him. As daylight turns to twilight in my room, blue and orange become the same gray, and I imagine that he is Oswald. Lying here, I miss his mewing, his licking, his fur, his warmth.

A Father's Advice

I. The Greatest Generation…
Speaks with a voice to be respected
Backed by a firm hand when boys will be boys
And "Mack the Knife" plays on the radio
And cuts up with a smile
All the while paving the future with memories
Praise, and unambiguous directions

Loving arms can hug a son in school
Only so long as a teen does not reciprocate
With a handshake, bought off by the "man mandate"
Growing moustache and beard, resistant and untouchable

II. Then…
The son departs from eternal brows of encouragement
And paternal wisdom which punctures the bull's eye
But not the piñata's head
That tissued cardboard veil that holds inside
Wrapped nuggets:
Nonpareils bordering right and wrong
Forbidden red licorice Twizzlers
And Tootsie Roll wounds that ooze
What friends said, and women did or didn't do

III. Instead…
The tapestry of conversation stays comfortable
Where inviting patterns lie plainly on the carpet
Like textured bark of Dogwood or Viceroy butterflies
That are easy to see when standing up and eye-to-eye

Fathers and sons can talk sunshine like that for years
Without seeing a bump as time slides and skitters by

IV. Soon…
Candy-loving children add charm to the pattern
With loving hearts and faces
And colors of fresh trees and flowers
Reaching for the sky
And so the conversation goes
Filled green with wandering ivy, work and envy
Proud achievements and minor problems
…Probing questions and pearls of wisdom
-- Considered but often pushed away

V. One day…
No surprise, really
The big green slide takes one down --
Face down to the carpet that burns
With the smell of feet passing over
And life passing by
It is the great Baby Boomerang
That strikes the back of the head
Rattling brain with unrelenting waves
Difficult to bear, more still, to share
Overwhelming spirit with a swimming feeling
That must swirl and sink
Or swim free

Looking up
Through the veil from the vortex below
There is an outstretched hand
Whose weathered skin and familiar heart
Was always there
Reaching across a generation
To what is and still can be
To claim a piece of himself deep within
With the knowingness and courage
Of a single mother raising paperboys
During the Depression
So long ago

VI. Now
Father sees son before him:
Reaches down to lift him up
And staunch the flow
With love and listening.

And the son grabs hold.

Author's Note:
Fathers seem to always be about the future, planning and thinking ahead for their families. Sons soon figure they can see far (enough) and can think for themselves. When life ensnares, sons do not want their fathers to see them in distress, and they do not want to endure criticism for (obvious) mistakes. Grabbing a fig leaf to hide behind seems preferable to grabbing a hand. Eventually, but not inevitably, maturity can change that and open a new world.

Note to Self

At 17, Zachary Revere was tall, lanky and slow to get out of bed. He was born in 1973 and his parents named him Zachary because it means God Remembers. But they always called their only child, Zach.

The teen groped for his contacts on the night table and yawned his way to the bathroom. His nearsightedness extended to his toothbrush but not much further. He leaned over the sink to insert his contacts. He always hated touching his eyeballs. When he finished, one contact wrinkled, and he had to blink to keep it flat.

With both eyes clear now, he was startled to see an old geezer, semi-transparent, standing behind him in a night-shirt. He was nearly as tall as Zach but hunched over, with thin, straggly hair a bright white. The ethereal figure said nothing. At first, Zach thought it was a ghost of his grandfather. Zach took a deep breath and found himself strangely relaxed. Was it an angel? Was he still sleeping?

Zach stared in the mirror, frozen, not wanting to turn around. A weird feeling swept through him: The old man wanted to communicate something. The man slowly raised his arms and held up a piece of etched glass with words in English that scrolled like a teleprompter. He could read them easily even though he was reading them in the mirror. It reminded Zach of when he first saw the word "Ambulance" in his rearview mirror -- but these words were moving.

Note to Self

1. ***Love and Beauty.*** Don't confuse these. Only when you see and feel the beauty within should you fall in love with her.

2. ***Relationships.*** Be genuine and strive to be kind. If you feel you cannot, move away from the person. Don't fake it.
3. ***Money.*** A.) Buy life insurance early. Think of it as saving your life when you are older, or others if your life is short. B.) When you first hear about Google and Facebook, buy baby buy.

Zach Revere still had his eyes closed. He had been in a coma for two weeks. His wife was long gone, but his five children and most of his grandchildren had come to visit him. He knew they were there, and it filled him with joy, even though he could not move. Last night they left, uncertain how long the coma might last.

At 6:08 a.m. the next morning, Zachary took his last breath. When the alarm went off at the nurses' station, the LPN and an intern came, but it was too late.

They had become acquainted with the family. The nurse spoke first: "It's sad. I liked him." "I don't think there was an angry bone in his body, and it shows on his face." She didn't say that about everyone. She sniffled and a tear dropped from her cheek. "All his children said he was such a devoted father, too. He was married for 52 years."

The intern agreed. "His son told me Mr. Revere had been highly successful. He sold life insurance, so I'm sure they'll all be well taken care of. His daughter mentioned he was also one of the original stockholders of Alphabet, when it first went public as Google in 2003. He became quite wealthy and started the Revere Trust for families suffering from mental illness. Ever hear of it?"

"Yes," she said. "What a remarkable man. It kind of makes you wonder how some people are so blessed. Do you think they know something we don't?"

The Diamond Affair

Nothing could go wrong. Although Buck McNeil did not get proper credit for the invention, he was chief bioelectronics engineer at International Express Transfer (IET) when the breakthrough came. It started with packages, then rats, dogs and chimps. Now 15 years later, virtual transfers were a $1.5 trillion industry. Simply by inserting your Global card in any booth and verifying the appropriate code, you could transfer yourself anywhere for a price--almost instantaneously.

Now Buck waited patiently in his rented office on the Australian countryside. He had spent a year planning this and had modified the software that controlled the transfer process himself. He glanced at his watch -- 2:59:12 (GMT). In less than a minute, Buck would see the Belgian diamond merchant appear. He gripped his anesthetic pistol and aimed through a hole in the wall of the booth.

Buck had to laugh. He knew Janssen would be expecting to appear at his bank at precisely 5 o'clock. What would he think when he was suddenly whisked away from the international diamond exchange in Munich and appeared in a strange office surrounded by over $50 million in cut diamonds? No, the Belgian would not even be stunned--he would hit the floor before he even knew what happened.

It was, in fact, quite remarkable that nothing had gone wrong with virtual transfers in their five years on the market. After almost a decade of testing and modifications, IET (now IVT, International Virtual Transfer) had created what seemed to be an impeccable system. Laminar sheets packing millions of bio-circuits had to be replaced weekly to maintain six nines reliability, 99.999999%. It cost only a fraction to fly, but virtual was instant and, theoretically, far safer.

The three primary R&D teams involved in the project were from divergent fields and coordination was a source of constant flare-ups. Peter Storkel, a biophysicist, was responsible for mapping the intricacies of biological processes. Charles Wexley, a mathematician, had to translate Storkel's findings into complex algorithms. And Buck McNeil's bioelectronics team, had to synch Wexley's algorithms with the bio-micron transformer/transmitter.

For a while, the development had gone smoothly, but the closer the team came to collating their findings, the more difficult the conversions—especially for McNeil. Thousands of circuits had to be combined to take the place of one. They found that at a micron-level gradient, matter, including biomatter would coalesce. Finally, when IVT made the announcement of the transfer booths public, only a team of scientists received credit for the construction of the booth. A single Norwegian physicist was credited with underlying the metaphysics. Ostensibly IVT was protecting its scientists by withholding their names and attributing the idea to a fictitious Norwegian. While it was fine for Storkel and Wexley (two hollow men in McNeil's opinion) to pocket $1 million and have their names revealed only after they were dead, McNeil wanted more—much more. If it was the reputation of the company that corporate officials worried about, well, McNeil would see to that.

* * *

Marc Janssen eyed his watch with impatience. Eight minutes late and still no sign of Sheik Abduhl. He had heard Arabs were difficult to deal with, but couldn't they at least be punctual? With the advent of virtual transfer there was no excuse for tardiness. 5:09:52. The Arab had promised superior color, cut and quality—large gems and lots of them. Could the sheik have found another buyer elsewhere? The uncertainty was irritating. But the prospect of seeing large, high-quality gems in quantity from an Arab sheik was something Janssen couldn't resist. He would have to quell his impatience.

* * *

111

At precisely 5:00:00 GMT, Buck McNeil fired a 50 ml shot of anesthetic through the hole he had bored through the plexiglass wall of the transfer booth. Although he had aimed precisely at what should have been Janssen's neck, the needle hit the opposite wall and fell to the floor. After six months of monitoring the Belgian's behavior, this was the first time Janssen had been late to the bank. McNeil unlocked the door to the transfer booth in his office and picked up his needle to reload.

* * *

Janssen took the leather pouch from the Arab and emptied its contents onto the white tissue paper he had unfolded on top of the table. It was difficult to disguise his awe as he examined the largest gem with his loupe. The 3.5 carat blue-white diamond sparkled like a chandelier, no flaws. All 36 diamonds were over 3 carats, blue-white, finely cut, each 168 points and full of fire. This was the most consistent batch he had seen in years. He must make the Arab an offer. He would have these diamonds.

The Belgian knew he could make a profit in New York if he could secure them at a reasonable price. But he must not appear too anxious. "I'll offer you $3.5M."

The sheik curled his lip. "Mr. Janssen, you know there is not a trace of yellow in these diamonds. They are of exceptional size and quality. I did not travel here to Antwerp to have you insult my intelligence. These diamonds are easily worth double that."

"Ahh, indeed Sheik Abduhl, I do not mean to insult you. They are of remarkably high quality, however, the most I can offer you is $5M."

The sheik's eyebrows twisted downward in disgust. "Mr. Janssen, you came highly recommended for your global connections, but if you did not want to deal with me, you should not have made the invitation. There are plenty of buyers here."

The Belgian eyed the diamonds again as if to reconsider. Yes, the sheik understood the quality, and oh, how Arabs liked to haggle.

Janssen would play the Arab's game. He could escalate the price to $6.5M and still garner three and a half percent on the resale after the cost of his virtual transfer to Manhattan—a fine profit on a deal this size. New York would pay 15 percent higher than Antwerp, and he knew the sheik was not welcome in the U.S. He looked the Arab in the eye.

"Perhaps you are right, Sheik Abduhl. These glisten like no others I have seen in weeks. I will raise my offer to $5.75M but I can go no higher."

Sheik Abduhl pounded the table and bared his yellowing, decaying teeth. He leaned forward so the Belgian could smell the garlic on his breath. "I am sorry we cannot do business."

"Now wait a second, Sheik." Janssen responded with a smile and a conciliatory tone. 'I'll offer you $6M—that's higher than I wanted to go."

The Arab weakened. At $6.25M, the pair sealed the deal with a handshake. Janssen transferred the funds, then walked toward his office with a quick tap to his side. The packet of diamonds was carefully tucked in the pocket of his gabardine jacket.

* * *

At IVT, an electronics engineer was monitoring the system control when he noticed a warning light flicker. Normally if there was a malfunction, the light would remain red, but it only lit once and stopped. Perhaps he hadn't seen it at all. No, Jacob Hurley had trained under Buck McNeil, and he knew better than to ignore his senses. He removed the cover to the control panel. Surely someone who had been studying electronics for eight years could figure out what caused the warning light. He pushed one end of a connector and found it loose. That was it. The indicator on the screen was now solid red. Circuit XKJ 19 was inoperative or malfunctioning.

Should he wait for McNeil to fix it? The chief electronics engineer would be at work in 32 minutes. No, a lot could happen in 32 minutes. If he left the system in a faulty state, it could be dangerous. If only one square micron of a person's brain tissue was misplaced in a transfer, it could alter the personality. Except for the heart and the brain, most other body tissue wasn't as critical, so perhaps he was getting excited over nothing.

Quickly, Hurley ran a system diagnostic and found a hidden problem that would be difficult to fix. Could there be others? --Perhaps the whole system was quietly malfunctioning. Maybe it had been malfunctioning ever so slightly in a way that no one had ever noticed. The thought startled him. Hurley called in his supervisor, Peter Storkel.

* * *

The diamond merchant peered into the lens of each camera at the four successive doors to his office. Janssen had enjoyed the cunning Arab's dealing and relished a moment of satisfaction at his own negotiating ability. 3:34:07. There was still time to make the drop at his safety deposit box before the bank closed.

He stepped into the transfer booth and secured the door from the inside. Inserting his card into the slot, he verified his ID and punched his code which began: XKJ 19---.

* * *

McNeil was growing impatient. He waited, poised for the moment he would see Janssen. He glanced at his watch: 3:35:00. If Janssen did not appear shortly, he would have to abort his plan.

Five million dollars was worth waiting for, especially if it meant destroying the reputation of IVT. It would only take a few moments to steal the diamonds and return Janssen back to his Belgian office—unconscious and empty-handed, but unharmed.

However, he still had to travel to his bank in Zurich and then to IVT. If he were more than 60 seconds late to work, he would arouse suspicion. His whole plan had depended on timing, and already Janssen was more than half an hour late. Would he come at all? . . .

As McNeil's thoughts flowed, for a fleeting moment, Janssen appeared. By the time McNeil fired his pistol, Janssen had vanished.

* * *

A strange feeling swept over the diamond merchant. For a fraction of a second after his finger touched the activating button, he felt he was somewhere else—somewhere foreign—not his bank. He hesitated for a moment, and then decided to take a cab across town rather than try again.

* * *

Whatever had gone wrong, McNeil did not like it. But there was little time for self-reproach. If he returned to IVT, he would still have time to adjust the settings before anyone noticed. Maybe he could find the mistake, and his heist would merely need to be rescheduled.

He tidied up the office and jumped into his IVT overalls. Perhaps the transfer booth which he had practically created single-handedly had a serious malfunction. Transferring people from place to place, instantaneously, was an impossibility when the world had been trapped into Einsteinian thinking. But what could have gone wrong? What happened to Janssen? Was he still alive? He had not meant to harm anyone.

McNeil inserted his card into the slot and punched KLX 21Q to take him to IVT. He paused for a moment. He was sure the system had been adjusted correctly, but perhaps there was something that he had overlooked.

* * *

Among IVT's banks of computers -- the brain of the transfer system -- Charles Wexley and Peter Storkel were making the final KLX readjustments. Circuits do not just cross-connect themselves they thought. There was only one explanation, and Peter Storkel knew exactly what to do.

There was a flurry of excitement when Buck McNeil arrived on the floor of IVT's busy office. The transfer booth was on a platform in the center of the room, so when McNeil slumped to the floor with a thud everyone noticed. The president of the company was nearby. He unlocked the door to the booth and helped McNeil out. Buck rose slowly to his feet with a curious gurgling sound.

The president asked what everyone wanted to know. "You all right, Buck? What happened?"

McNeil did not respond directly. His body was numb. His thoughts were muddled--devoid of words. There was only movement, sound, color and people. He listened to the strange sounds that fell from the lips of this man. McNeil tried to speak but could only drool and make guttural sounds as his eyes rolled around in their sockets.

Author's Note:
I wrote this in the age before the Internet, before desktop computers, when people still made calls from phone booths. The year was 1977, and the story was for a science mini-course at Rutgers titled, "Physics: Fact or Fiction." It was taught by a motorcycle-riding physicist (who liked the story better than the reductionist science). --I made only minor modifications for this book.

Upside Down:

Stories from the edge…
The horizon, a precipice for ships
Seems so far away
But then we descend a winding staircase
We were supposed to ascend
And we find ourselves with vertigo
Looking up
When we should be looking out
From a lighthouse
To signal a warning

Dancing She Remembers

Mother's black loafers shuffle and burn a circle
Around the living-and-dying room floor
And the kitchen
Encircling recipes and past dreams
Filed away forever

Dying in eternity present
Flash-freezing relations,
Dear husband, children, friends,
Words waterfall
Streaming with and without meaning

Yet between phonemes
Emotions swim still
Phrases trip on a threshold, "Jesus Christ"
Instinctively, you hug her
She hugs back
A beaming smile blurts "I *Love* you"

Boogie-woogie eyes
You switch on Benny Goodman, 40s swing
She cuts a circle "In the Mood" carpet
Then Sinatra serenades
Midnight's candle
Flickering low

Dancing she remembers
An eternal moment captured long ago
Now in a teardrop
That touches the floor

Author's Note:
Familiar music is always good therapy… The number of U.S. adults over age 40 living with dementia is projected to rise from 5.2 million people in 2019 to 10.5 million by 2050. Source: The Lancet.[6]

---

[6] Open Access Published January 6, 2022 DOI: https://doi.org/10.1016/S2468-2667(21)00249-8
"Estimation of the global prevalence of dementia in 2019 and forecasted prevalence in 2050: an analysis for the Global Burden of Disease Study 2019," Nichols, Emma et al., The Lancet Public Health, Volume 7, Issue 2, e105 – e125

No Firm Ground

There was something William Waverly had forgotten but didn't want to remember. He had been a successful architect for an engineering firm in Georgia and had retreated to California after the accident.

Had he locked the door to his house? The thought nagged him as he drove across The Golden Gate on this windy Wednesday. The cables seemed to jangle like Slinkys. Was it the just wind? He fought the feeling. The roadway felt wavy, but vehicles were still driving straight. No one was honking. He wondered about the quality of the stranded steel cables.

On the other side, he spotted Alcatraz chiseled beneath muddy clouds. Aboard a tall ship, sailors in black-and-white who could be prisoners waved their arms as they adjusted the sails. He cracked his window near the wharf, and the smell of fish penetrated his nostrils. Dozens of seals barked. On the sidewalk, a woman in a red scarf worked to restrain her barking dalmatian.

Waverly wheeled right, remembering the path to the office. Pastel homes zipped by, uphill and down, until his stomach threatened. He parked a block away, set the brake and stepped carefully to avoid hazards pushing up the sidewalk.

After a long wait, Dr. Schwartz invited him in. The hushed room sunk in dim light, two deep chairs opposite one another, a pool of blue rug between them. The clock chimed 10 times before the doc asked. Waverly admitted he felt shaky, and the thought that he had forgotten something important gripped him.

"It wasn't your fault, Willy."

I'm not sure, so how can you be?

"Your firm made you a scapegoat. They turned you out. But the matter was investigated for two years. The court found the liability belonged to the construction team. You were exonerated."

That building should not have collapsed. Fifty-four people died.

"Yes, it was a tragedy. But you need to understand that if the construction team used substandard concrete, that was their fault, not yours."

The next Wednesday, Mr. Waverly had a breakthrough: He remembered a memo he had drafted advising the construction manager that the specification for the concrete foundation should be improved to M60 for added safety.

"And you communicated it. So where's the problem?"

M50 was the correct design mix per industry standards, but I wanted it higher.

"So that's why your firm singled you out?"

Yes, they buried the memo after the accident. I tried to find it in my files the next day, but it was gone. The construction manager said he never received it -- and didn't know what I was talking about. In fact, all the people I copied right up to the VP of operations, insisted they never saw it.

"You're sure you sent it then?"

Don't you see? It was a coverup. They gaslighted me -- then pushed me out for 'performance issues.' They destroyed my reputation, and my confidence.

Dr. Schwartz said Willy should feel a burden lifted since he now knew the truth.

The cables of the Golden Gate jangled like Slinkys.

He felt relief as he returned to his Volvo and headed back to Sonoma. Yet halfway over the bridge, the cables started bouncing vigorously, and now the bridge swayed with a slight twisting motion. Cars started to drift lanes and skid. A double-decker bus barreled toward him. He swerved to avoid it. His heart surged, but he kept his hands on the wheel.

Mr. Waverly reached the other side unscathed. Yet on the long ride home, he wondered again: Had he recalled it correctly, or was there something else important he should remember?

Purple Dragon

Eva Langhorn teased Martin Green for sport in grade school. She'd say he was weirder than a Cheshire cat, his nose resembled a turnip, and his eyes shined like Jupiter. Martin would cringe every time he looked in the mirror. The playground was the worse. She'd hang upside down on the monkey bars, her piercing eyes tracking him like lasers. Whenever he'd glance over, she'd twist her face in disgust.

That's when Dougie's visits began. He had a friendly voice and a sinuous blue tail that punctuated his words. The purple dragon would perch on Martin's shoulder whenever he felt down. And he was feeling down a lot lately. Dougie would usually just cajole Martin until he felt better. But today, he asked Martin to do one small thing.

Eva was swinging high, bragging she was going to swing over the top until the chains wound around the top rail. Martin was standing just behind watching her swing back and forth. Then she started jerking the chains. Suddenly, she was sitting on the ground.

Instinctively, Martin grabbed the heavy swing and pulled it back a little. *"Now let go,"* Dougie whispered.

The swing caught Eva in the head. She was rushed away and returned the next day with a few stitches. The teacher had called Martin's mother that night. He explained that "It just slipped." Dougie cheered him up and told him to forget about it.

By high school, Martin wasn't totally sure if he still hated Eva Langhorn, or if he secretly liked her. It didn't matter. She was so beautiful she was just a fantasy.

Martin enjoyed Dougie so much that he didn't need other friends. Long before Martin had graduated from Fair Lawn High, Dougie taught him never to feel bad about anything. When his mother died of lung cancer his junior year, Martin discovered he could cry tears without pain. Dougie always encouraged him: *"You're a man of steel."*

It had been a few years since he had thought of Eva. After community college, Martin took a job in New York City as an accounting clerk and moved to Garfield, N.J. He'd take the A train to 23rd and walk three blocks to his office, which gave him enough time for a last smoke. At 5 p.m., he'd put a menthol between his lips and head for the subway to Port Authority Bus Terminal.

Today the subway was taking forever. He peered up the tunnel searching for light. He played with his lighter, wondering how much longer. Dougie counseled *patience.*

Martin took a step back from the yellow warning zone. A moment later, he saw her approaching: She wore a blue dress with diamond earrings, and her red hair bounced with every step. Martin edged toward her as the platform continued to fill. Something welled up in him, and he felt warm under the collar. *"Move closer, Martin. She won't bite."* Martin wasn't so sure. He searched the tunnel again, noticing lights reflecting from the steel rails.

As the train drew closer, he could hear Dougie's voice over the din: *"Go ahead, be brave."*

Everyone was inching forward as the wheels screeched around the last bend. Martin shuffled forward until he stood directly behind her. Her pumps pushed into the yellow zone, and her perfume filled Martin's nostrils. The train rattled to a stop with a hiss of the airbrakes.

"Thrilling, isn't it?" Dougie whispered.

Maybe she'll get a second chance, but don't count on it...

The crowd surged forward as the doors opened, sweeping Eva and Martin in together. Dougie chimed in with eternal optimism: *"Maybe you'll get another chance."*

The subway was packed. Eva grabbed the aluminum pole with her right hand, and Martin grabbed just above with his left. Their bodies were now facing, though Eva's head was turned. "Eva Langhorn," he said aloud. It was not a question so much as a statement.
She twisted her neck around. Her face crinkled as she brought him into focus and smiled. "Martin Green? I'd recognize that face anywhere."

Martin noted the comment, but let it pass. "--Even in a packed subway station," he said.

"What a strange coincidence meeting you here."

The irony was not lost on Dougie who snickered.

"Strange indeed," Martin answered. "I work at a Big 3 accounting firm on 8th. What about you, Eva?" He liked the way her name sounded on his lips. Her brown eyes sparkled with flecks of yellow he never noticed before. She seemed genuinely happy to see him.

"It's funny. I just had my first interview at Mizzy, and they offered me a job as account manager. They're a top agency for women's apparel. I start Monday. I'm so excited," she beamed.

"Congratulations, *Eva.* "Martin felt a tinge of jealousy but didn't let it surface. "We should celebrate. I know an Irish pub by Radio City that makes a mean Brunswick stew." He couldn't believe the words flowing effortlessly.

Dougie interjected, *"Good one, my lad."*

"Oh, I really couldn't," she said. "I have to catch the 6:09 and get back home."

"Where's home?"

"Still in Fair Lawn."

"Me too," Martin answered. "You take the 164?"

"That's the one."

"Me too. We can take the 8:09 back together." For a moment he imagined how nice it would be to sit next to her on the bus, her thigh against his. --"What do you say?"

"Tonight's laundry night."

"Ouch," Martin said aloud, echoing Dougie's sentiment with a crestfallen look.

"It's true. I've got a pile as high as the Statue of Liberty. I didn't mean to hurt you. I'm sorry."

"Well, your laundry can wait. You really need to get out and celebrate. All we have to do is take the No. 7 to Grand Central and the D to Rockefeller Center."

Martin detected a sense of pity as Eva studied him for a long moment. "Ok," she finally said, "Just don't think this means we're going to be lifelong friends or anything."

"Bingo!" Dougie whispered.

"I can assure you of that," Martin responded. The strain in her voice surprised him -- and stung in a way he hadn't felt in some time. It reminded him of a long-forgotten detail: Whenever Eva winced from the monkey bars, her tongue shot out a final barb. (Why was he asking her to dinner?) Dougie remained silent now, but Martin already knew the answer.

"Do you believe in second chances?" Martin asked.

Take a Ride with Jake

JAKE: To tell ya the truth, it scares me a little. People move just too-o *damn* slow. They like to make you wait, then they eat your time like an all-day sucker. You wait in line for groceries, for customer service, for somebody to pick up the phone. The government's the worst. They don't even answer -- and my beard's growing to my knees waitin' for my tax refund.

Outta my way, Mac. I'll drive you through those Golden Arches!... See that?

Don't these people know I gotta get where I'm going? I make my money, and I have a right to spend it how I want. But time's a-wasting, people. Ya just gotta put the pedal to the metal...

Now move, ya old buzzard. Trade it in for a wheelchair! HONK!...

Can you believe this? --A U-Haul in the left lane? *Get back. Slugs and suckers over there...*

Seems to me slow is spreading like jam on toast. Some places may be thicker, but it's everywhere, and it gets messy.

If you don't move sister, I'm going around. Vroom right, vroom left. Now eat my exhaust!

Watch this...

Hey, baby cheeks. Who bought you that fancy minivan? Rich bitch with the squealing kids in the back, I'm cutting you off. --And your bumper can kiss mine... See that?

Everyone and everything is slow. Even fast food. The only thing moving fast is the price of gas. Drives me to drink... Oh, look at this moron...

Why is Jake in such a hurry?

You left your left blinker on. --Now hard left into the guardrail. HONK!

Idiots always look better in my mirror.

OK, Let me by you, ya fat pig! Ready for the market? I'm FIRST. Now get over. HONK!

Jake screeches into a space in front of the ABC store. He waits an eternity for the cashier but figures he can still make it if he hurries. He emerges with a liter of Jack Daniels, ready to race to the beach. And...he gets there just in time...

The next day at work, Jake swears to anyone who'll listen that the reds and oranges across the sky made it the best sunset he'd ever seen.

Blue Paradise

Hold me close
Let love surround us
Let us bathe in a tropical blue paradise.

There is love
That pounds deep in our hearts,
Love that sees all things from here to eternity.

But lightning flashes in our eyes.
We live inside the curling of the wave.
The sea swells and rocks us through the night.
The storm stretches us *incommunicado*
… On and on and on and on.
There are reasons that start so deep,
Good reasons that see things from here to eternity.

(Chorus)
Hold me close
Let love surround us
Let us bathe in a tropical blue paradise.

Until forgiveness dawns again.
Breaking stripes across the sky,
To heal our wounds and to salt our lives.
Two birds soaring on the morning wind,
Sliding across the breeze…
Sliding on and on and on … and on.

(Chorus)
(Instrumental)
(Chorus)
There is love
That pounds deep in our hearts,
Love that sees all things from here to eternity…

Author's Note:

I wrote this as lyrics for an instrumental by Santana titled, "El Farol," on the 15X platinum album, *Supernatural*, released in 1999. It's one of the best-selling albums in the world (over 30 million copies) and features the hit single, "Smooth."

Daniel the Statue

Is the man in the hospital gown really a statue? No, people are just too fast, passing blurs speaking munchkin. His silent mantra: *Stop disease!*

Sloth-like, he moves almost im-per-cep-ti-bly. Right hand's poised strangely, above his forearm; no, *moo-ving*, fingers cupping, downward. Why? Nothing there...

Until it appears, cling-ing to the short hairs of his wrist. The mosquito probes once. ...Sixty-seven minutes later, Daniel's ingested it. The staff see a statue still.

Author's Note:

I found a literary website that only publishes stories of 75 words or less, including the title. This is exactly that. However, they don't publish illustrations, so I never submitted it. ... By eliminating flying pests, the man is performing an important and potentially life-saving function for the hospital.

DUNKIN'

It kinda makes ya think
'Donut'
Don' it?

Author's Note:
I wrote this in 2012 – long before the famous donut franchise shortened its name.

Fear of the Bagman

Marty Marchesi was a driver for 'Uncle Vinnie' now, and life was good. He'd tried construction, but with a wife and kids, it just wasn't enough. He was always afraid of losing his job, of being lost in the jungle of New York City. Then he got laid off.

When Marty was four, his father lost him at a carnival. He froze for what seemed *hours*. Then like fog condensing, his father appeared, smiling back. Raised Catholic, Marty had loved his father, even though he didn't see him much. By the time he was seven though, when his father did come around, he turned into a bull.

After Marty's 9th birthday, his father backhanded his mom, raising an ugly welt. He left them crying and never came back. But Marty's anxiety did, and never really subsided until he started driving. Uncle Vinnie treated Marty like his own blood, said he could earn a monthly bonus.

At first the Lower East Side felt scrambled, alien; but after a few weeks, Marty felt like he belonged. It was 4:10 p.m., and Quentin's bodega on Houston St. was his last stop. He'd double park, pick up the cash, then head home to play catch with Tommy.

Quentin owed $300--late three weeks running, and Marty was doing the Christian thing not charging interest. But Marty needed to collect if he hoped to earn his bonus. Intimidation energized Marty because he hated to lose, hated feeling adrift. He grabbed the Billy bat off the seat and patted his .38.

The supermarket sat below grade, three rows wide, register up front, stockroom in back. Marty clicked down the steps, then glared at Quentin, bat rat-a-tat-tatting the counter. An Asian couple skittered out the front. "Got something for me, Quent?"

"Business is slow. You know that."

The bat struck the counter. "Wha'cha gonna do 'bout it?"

"I need more time."

The bat cracked the Formica. Quentin winced.

"Tell me your register's empty, and I'll hobble you."

"I owe suppliers so I can stay open and pay you."

The hair on Marty's neck prickled. Another crack. "*Open the register!*"

Quentin hesitated. "Isn't there another way?"

Marty snatched a breath, rat-a-tat-tatting to consider: *Protection wasn't Vinnie's only racket; he'd appreciate Marty stepping up.* "What about that teenager of yours? I bet he's got tons of friends in school."

"I can't involve him."

"Then open the *damn* register."

The drawer sprang open. Marty sprawled across the counter, leaned over and started stuffing fistfuls of cash in his shirt with his outstretched hand. As he worked, Quentin backed away, then sidestepped behind a post. He glanced at the doorway to the back. "Don't do it!"

His son was leveling a double-barreled shotgun at Marty's head.

The bagman slowly turned. "You're not gonna shoot me, kid."

"I will if you don't do exactly what I say. Drop the cash and move away."

Marty emptied the top of his shirt; bills falling behind the counter like leaves. Slowly, he pushed back and let his feet slide to the floor, knowing his derringer could easily waste the boy. *But there were lots of ways to lose here: He never shot anyone and didn't want the kid on his conscience. He was a bag man, not a killer, just selling protection to businesses that needed it. Plus, Uncle Vinnie hated messes.*

He kept his eye on the teen and backed toward the steps. Reaching the landing, he grinned with a jerk of his chin: "Glad you didn't kill anybody today, kid? --I am." Then he looked the store owner in the eye: "Next week, Quent. --Nobody needs a fire."

Back in his Dodge Charger, Marty pulls $300 from his billfold and drops it in the collection pouch, confident of his bonus.

Clam Up

Was it something I said,
Just a tiny bit of sand
insinuating its way
between your lips
That crack of day
Only to clam up
Once inside
To hide what you feel?

Or a chance to congeal
To listen instead
To the dance in your head
To that endless
    intoxicating tone
That echoing breath
    of being alone
To lie at the bottom of the sea
Waiting for something
    to change
Could it be me?
That bit of sand
Was it love, or
    encouragement lost,
Request or impossible
    demand,
A future at towering cost?
Not in your Opinion
(Ocean of dominion)
But a canard, a line crossed,
A Word, not yours, but mine
That swapped hope for hell
For heaven to be resigned
To living life blind
Inside a shell so fine,

So smooth and hard,
Comfortable and irritating,
To you and to me

That bit of sand
It does fester and grow
It's inside you, but I feel it, too
A kernel of past to
    heal and regain
With time embracing
As tides pass by slowly
Dark storms sweep through
Over me and you

A heart endures through pain
Deems to keep smoothing
And polishing that bit of sand
Forever so it seems

Until one swoops down
Searching with
    outstretched hand
Pushing, holding his breath
For as long as he believes
That mollusk bubbles
    and breathes
And the clam it will open
To reveal a pearl
Be it black, gray or white
And it will be the finest sight.

Sunrise Sonata

It was the same, every day. Each morning before sunrise, Nelson Chalmers would read the 23rd Psalm from the Bible on his night table. Then he would shower, get dressed and select a button-down shirt from his closet. Next, he'd open the top drawer of his dresser, take the tattered Bible with the hole in it, and tuck it in his breast pocket. After shutting the door behind him, he'd shuffle to the lounge area and wait in a recliner for sunup and his morning paper.

A Vietnam Vet, Nelson had had lived a decent life, though his wife of 45 years died two years ago. He was never a solid sleeper, but now he had COPD and his cough often woke him before the alarm clock. He was thankful his mind was still essentially intact, though he knew paperwork could confuse him and he needed help with his pills.

After Sandra died, his son Carl, the CPA, convinced him Sunrise Sonata would be the best place for him. But Carl did not visit often, and most of the people were in worse shape than him, so the Sonata could, at times, be depressing and lonely. Memories, good and bad, often eluded Nelson, and they could sometimes haunt, and occasionally surprise him. A few minutes after the sun came up, Nelson would close his eyes until, sometime later, an attendant named Marcus would bring him the newspaper.

His eyes were open wide now. He stared at a coil of rope on the floor and gave his left pocket a tap. His mind squelched the fear and the chop-chop-chop of the blades of the Chinook. They were one of many in the swarm that included Hueys and Cobras that morning. A salty breeze blew across his cheeks, and he imagined a boy digging across the sand pulling a string with a box kite that darted in the wind. Was he holding the string or his son, Carl? He wasn't sure anymore. The boy let out more string and the kite soared higher.

The spiral of rope at his feet seemed to swirl now, and he took no notice of the men standing shoulder-to-shoulder next to him in the chopper. Instead, he imagined an Indian with a turban sitting cross-legged in front of the coiled rope blowing a lilting tune on a flute. A small crowd had gathered to watch. Nelson always wanted to go to someplace far away like India, but the Army said different. As if entranced by the melody, the rope seemed to rise into the air, yet it was not the rope, but a Cobra swaying back and forth, ready to strike.

The moment with the snake charmer fell away and stretched into a desert where the twisted arms of an elm reached for the clouds trying to find purchase. Below the elm, a Mexican wearing chaps and a sombrero sat astride a horse, hands bound behind him, a noose around his neck. "Help me. Help me, gringos."

Nelson wanted to help the man. Yet the Mexican was not talking to him but rather to two cowboys riding away on horseback, one with a black hat, the other white. It was a scene from "The Good, the Bad, and the Ugly." It comforted Nelson that he knew what would happen next, even though the horse would get antsy. From a distance, Clint Eastwood, in poncho and light hat, would stop to watch chewing his cigar. After a moment, he'd pull his Winchester, carefully aim and fire. The rope frays. The second shot cuts the man free.

There is the rope at his feet again. Nelson wonders if it will take him up to heaven this time instead of down.

The top of the rope is clipped to the ceiling, two ropes on either side of the chopper. "Now, Now, Now!" the sergeant barks. Each man does as they're told, repelling down into the tall grass. This is the LZ, the landing zone Cambodia in the dawn of the Tet counteroffensive.

Sliding down, Nelson feels a thump, then a fire in his ribs. He lands hard and tumbles but cannot find his feet. As he lays on his back, he sees his platoon buddies scattering away in the tall grass. But Jonesy, the man behind him on the rope, stops and kneels by his side.

"You ok, Nelson?"

Nelson looks from Jonesy's eyes to the orange sky and back again unable to speak. He taps his chest – unable to catch his breath.

Bullets whiz overhead. "What?" Jonesy demands. Then he notices that Nelson's breast pocket sports a hole.

An eternity passes. Finally, Nelson's breath returns. "I'm hit, lost my wind, but I think I'm ok." Jonesy helps him up.

The round stopped short and lodged in his left rib just above his heart. They laughed about it later.

The sunrise is an extraordinary watercolor. After the spectacle, he dozes. He's awakened by a familiar voice. "And how are you this morning, Mr. Chalmers?" Marcus, the morning attendant, leans in and puts the Sunday *USA Today* in Nelson's hand. Nelson glances at the date. He smiles wider than Marcus can remember. "Today is my birthday, Marcus."

"Well happy birthday, then."

"My son is visiting." Nelson hadn't heard from Carl in months but hoped he would surprise him.

Marcus remembered what happened last year. "Don't get your hopes up too high, Mr. Chalmers."

Nelson had shuttered that memory and refused the possibility. "He'll be here. Don't you worry, Marcus." He tapped his shirt pocket. "Either way, I'm blessed."

At 9:15 a.m. a call came to the front desk. Marcus patted Nelson on both shoulders. "Happy birthday again, Mr. Chalmers. You are doubly blessed today. Carl just called to say he and Samantha will be here at 2:30 this afternoon with your first grandchild."

Harbor

The tide stems the flow, but cannot stop it:

Waves lap aimlessly against her hull
Sycophantic rhythms covering the cries of ghosts
Who loved their wenches and leapt aboard,

Short knives a-tooth, broadswords sweeping
At the claps of the blunderbuss
Greeting great courage and folly.

A winking lighthouse and harbor beckon
Curving light inward with encrusted memories
As tattered sails and mizzenmast emerge.

A tourniquet is lashed to her mainmast
To save it from splintering.
The tide stems the flow but cannot stop it.

Anger and desire, love and treasure, roil in the sun;
Blood spattering wheelhouse walls,
Shuffling madness and time.

Floorboards slick with algae
Feel the weight of shifting feet and cargo
Seeking balance over waves of emotions.

The hold catches reverie billows of cannon fire
But doesn't see the ball that rips in return,
Cracking beam and bones of men.

Yet the yardarm recalls quivering lips and pleas
Of cherry pirates spit out to sea for sharks
On their downward plunge.

Rats chew hard when a storm stomps in;
The anchor frays. Is the tourniquet loose?
The tide stems the flow, but cannot stop it:

Anger and desire, love and treasure, roil in the sun;
Blood spattering wheelhouse walls,
Shuffling madness and time.

*

Time now obscures the bloodstained deck
In rain-sodden wood slowly decaying.

As the woodworm burrows for safety,
Women in white hats and parasols pass by
Imbibing the majesty of Her masculinity,
Unaware of nibbling rats ready to board.

Just Another Day? *Not!*

It started out like any other day. I hit the snooze button three times before I got out of bed, shaved and jumped in the shower. On my way to the fridge, however, I tripped over a dog toy then stumbled forward and stubbed my toe. My day descended rapidly from there.

While I was making eggs and bacon, my chihuahua, Frankie, was barking, and I called to my son, George, who was not yet up. I had to go to his bedroom to coax him. When I returned to the stove the eggs were burned.

As we were headed out the door five minutes late, I didn't notice it until it was too late. Frankie left me a present on the floor. It took another five minutes to clean my shoe.

I stopped at the school to drop Georgie off, and he tells me he has something he wants to share, but "Don't get mad, Dad," he says. He hands me a math test with a D+ at the top. "Thank God I passed," he says. "I need your signature." There was not time to argue.

On the last turn before work, a pickup cuts me off, sending me skidding. I missed a tree but was a little shaky when I got to the office.

Since I was 15 minutes late, I tried to sneak past the boss' office. "Samson, you're late again. Don't forget we have that conference call at 9:30 am. You better be prepared."

"Sorry, I'm late, sir. I'll be ready." Of course, I really thought I would prepare when I got to work 10 minutes early. Instead, I was still a bit frazzled and fumbled through my part of the presentation with our biggest client. They were not impressed, and I felt awkward and embarrassed. The boss told me I could leave the room after I finished presenting.

Back at my desk, I tried to get my mind on the next piece of business, but my emotions were everywhere, and my head was swimming.

A half hour later, the boss calls me into his office and tells me how disappointed he is in me. He said the client wanted me off the account, and that meant that he could no longer employ me.

On the way home, another pickup cut me off. My son didn't have much to say after school. We ate burgers while watching TV, and I went to bed early.

The next day, when I heard the alarm clock go off, I hit the snooze button three times, took my son to school then returned home. I decided that today would be different. I put my pajamas back on and stayed in bed during a thunderstorm. And wouldn't you know, a tree crashed on our house.

I guess it's like the saying goes, cheer up, things could get worse. So I started singing "The Star-Spangled Banner" and it made me feel better. Of course, when I looked up the sky spit in my face and *Oh, say could I see* -- a branch reaching down from my bedroom ceiling.

Now I'm singing "You've Really Got a Hold on Me."

Red Wagon

The red wagon by the bushes at the edge of the yard reminds Madeline of her childhood. She peers from behind a live oak at the edge of the park across the street, musing and pulling her sweater tight.

She certainly didn't expect to see it, but it is there. The wagon that belonged to the little blonde-haired girl named Molly. A hiker found her wrapped in a shower curtain; she had drowned in a bathtub. --No, the wagon couldn't be the same, Madeline decides. It's in the same place, but it isn't at all rusty as she remembers. It is brand new a year later. Molly's mother must want to see it from the window.

Today is Madeline's 33rd birthday and looking at the wagon on this blustery autumn day somehow makes her feel warm. She imagines it is Molly's birthday, too. Four was a decent age, Madeline thinks, smart enough to know what's going on even if you couldn't remember it all -- "but smart enough to keep your mouth shut," as Madeline's mother would always say.

Madeline's mother would pull the arm of her easy chair and lay all the way back blowing smoke rings and staring at the ceiling. Madeline would climb into her lap and watch the rings expand and spread into nothing. Her mother would stroke Madeline's dark locks absentmindedly with one hand while she set her cigarette down and lifted the bottle to her lips.

Madeline experienced moments of comfort there. She smelled the blend of menthol and cinnamon whiskey on her mother's breath as she nestled into her bosom and started to drift off.

A gust of wind rustles the canopy above her head, and blotches of color dance to the ground. She rubs one of the small white circles on the back of her hand, the one nearest her thumb. That was the day Madeline was climbing into her mother's lap and her doll's hand knocked the lamp. Her mother screamed and jerked as the lamp fell, knocking her bottle and crystal ashtray onto the tile.

After it happened, there was a foul smell. Her mother snarled wrapping the band-aid: "Don't ever tell your father. And if he asks, tell him it was an accident."

Madeline settles again on the red wagon. With a flick of her thumb, she lights up a smoke. She closes her eyes and recalls the sweet fragrance of strawberry shampoo in Molly's hair. She exhales slowly and promises herself she will always come back to this place on her birthday.

Author's Note:
I originally wrote this as a Halloween mystery for *Cape Fear Voices.* The drawing of Madeline was one of my first since learning that it is easy to draw cartoons if you start with two sixes for eyes.

Two Ways to Break a Record

Guinness's Book is filled with feats of derring-do
Triumphs and challenges everyone wants to hear
Strongest, fastest, grandest, *whew!*
Champions of sports, year after year

And don't forget lesser-known wannabees
Winners of dance marathons and Frisbees
Pie- and dog-eating contests
New names and epithets
Records of amazing memory and longevity
Paul Bunyan strength, Tom Thumb brevity
-- It's enough to make your mind go silent.

But there's another record you can't get around
Someone you know, perhaps, a voice, so strident
A long-playing record on a loop--a god-awful sound

Words that pour out fire and acid rain
Spitting pieces of sorrow and pain
Replaying old movies again and again
Seeing conspiracy in everyone's game
Everyone -- the source of all blame

Sharing only means to chew everyone's ear
Letting them bleed out 'til the next leap year
Fear of abandonment bites friends in the face
Breaks the arms of those who might embrace
It seems there's no letting go, no chance to forget
No chance of forgiveness, to unburden debt
Only a boil festering with brokenness

A mouth streams daggers of damage long since past
Yet for those who believe in hope, the die is not cast
There's a door if these hoarders could just see the catch
All they have to do is listen -- and blow out the match.

Robin Hood

Since I've retired, one of my favorite pastimes is watching people -- and they can surprise you. I was a janitor by trade, but always fancied myself an amateur sleuth, unassuming like Columbo.

Last week when the weather was nasty, I went to Walmart for socks. While I'm in the men's department, I spot this character with a stubbly beard wearing a trench coat and sneakers, pushing a cart with just a package of T-shirts.

I'm spying him through the racks rummaging the underwear display where I had just browsed. He's spending too much time. Then I see him snatch some briefs. Instead of putting them in his basket, he deposits them inside his coat. Did I really just see that?

I make an arc and start looking at shirts about 20 ft. behind him. He bends over and picks up a package from the bottom shelf where the boy's underwear is. This time I see him clearly and he's got two packages. It makes me start to wonder about this guy, mid-30s, a bit straggly. His coat has a smudge on the left elbow. Does he have a job? What's his game?

Next, he wanders over to women's lingerie and starts thumbing through the underwear. He wasn't interested in the bras, just undies. Maybe he's married, a girlfriend perhaps, with a birthday? No, he must be married if he's picking up boy's underwear, too. Sure enough, he grabs three pair--pink, black and nude, and stuffs them inside his coat. A young woman in her twenties then enters the department shopping bras. That's when "Rodney" heads for the exit.

I'm 20 paces behind holding three pairs of socks wondering if he'll pay. He gets in line but only pays for the one package in his cart, with cash. I pay cash, too, so I can trail him. Door security checks his receipt. Outside, he saunters to a 2007 Toyota with a loose bumper. I note the plate.

I might've ratted him out, but my curiosity's screaming: What's his story? Does he have a family? Is he holding people hostage, and if so, why would he care about their underwear?

At the traffic light, Rodney turns and parks in front of the Salvation Army store. He gets out carrying the Walmart bag, now stuffed, into the store. When I enter, he's already at the counter asking for the manager. Nonchalantly, I start flipping through the men's golf shirts. (I always get a good deal in the off season.)

Finally, the manager emerges, and Rodney hands her the bag with seven unopened packages of underwear. "I'd like to make a donation," he announces. He doesn't want a receipt.

Quickly, I hang up a cool shirt and scurry out, my curiosity ready to pounce.

I confront him by his Toyota. "Sir, can I ask you a question? --I saw what you did…"

"I like to be generous," he answers.

"No, not here; at Walmart."

"I wasn't at Walmart," he lies.

That's what it said on your bag."

"Glad you can read. I gotta go."

No, really. *You* have to tell me, or I have to tell someone.

He looks me in the eye. "Keep a secret?"

Unblinking, I nod.

"Two years ago, I lost my job and my house. Now I'm getting on my feet."

"So why all the underwear?"

"Well, if you're homeless, next to socks, underwear's the most important thing in the world."

"Did you have to purloin them?"

"I'm still climbing out of a hole, but there's folks that need this stuff more 'n me. They can't wait."

"Thanks for your honesty," I said as his door creaked shut.

I went back inside, bought the golf shirt, then donated it with my new socks.

Author's Note:
If you steal, you could get arrested and lose your freedom and self-respect. Of course, if you steal in the Middle East, you could lose everyone's respect—and your hand. But what if you're hungry? Assuming *you* are not hungry, consider giving generously to the food banks in your area.

It Would Only Take a Second

It would only take a second. It wouldn't be a crime exactly, but it would violate a code of conduct he was sworn to uphold, a code drummed into him through 30 weeks of training and practiced assiduously the past 15 month on the job, a job he was specially selected for through extended family connections.

Yes, it would only take a second. She could, of course, get him fired, and all of that training, this special position he had worked for and been so fortunate to achieve would evaporate. He would be cast back into obscurity, drudging away again in his father's print shop.

Yes, it would only take a second. His parents might be disappointed in him if they actually witnessed the moment. But the sun was at his back and the bearskin hat would cast a shadow. Even though the event was being televised around the world, all eyes would be on her.

Yes, it would only take a second. How long had he waited to see her again in person? Of course, he saw her every day taped to the inside of his locker, her dark hair flowing around her high cheeks. Her beauty, captured in an ornate frame, also adorned his bedroom desk, igniting warm pride and yearning with every glance. Indeed, he had thought about her, pined for her every day, well before his fortune put him in this position.

Yes, it would only take a second. The moment was almost here as he watched the procession approaching the church, the gilded carriage holding the bride to be. And why did this red festooned groom have to marry her? So they could live a life of pomp and fortuitous circumstance, no doubt.

Yes, it would only take a second. Though who was he anyway? A lowly foot soldier performing a duty that was nothing more than pageantry and tradition. He wanted to gaze at his boots to see his reflection in their mirrored finish, but he dared not look down.

Yes, it would only take a second. The couple would soon disembark from the gilded carriage. He was one of the few soldiers who would stand this close as she passed.

Yes, it would only take a second. He stood at attention. The carriage approached slowly, only footsteps away. His neck moved not a muscle, but his smiling eyes slid gently sideways, and he winked.

Yes, it only took a second. --And it was worth it. Beautiful Kate, Princess of Wales, had smiled back.

Photo credit: Travis Gilbert

What moment could he be waiting for?

Author's Note:
I finished the first draft of this story just before King Charles' 2023 coronation. I originally envisioned the setting as Princess Kate Middleton's 2011 wedding and was planning to use a generic photo of the Queen's Guard. However, I decided to change that after visiting a craft fair in mid-May at Legacy Architectural Salvage in Wilmington, N.C. Coincidentally, I overheard Travis Gilbert, executive director of Historic Wilmington Foundation, talking about the coronation. He had camped in a tent for three days so he could hopefully catch a glimpse of Princess Kate. "When the carriage passed," he said, "she turned and looked straight at me. --Wanna see my money shot?"

Getting to the Point (A Valuable Lesson)

Straining to hear the Sunday sermon
Gulliver leans way over and down low
But does brush against a sycamore bow
And upsets a hive, and a particular mad bee.

And don't you suppose, in no mood to play,
The bee stings the giant in the nose.
Before he can think, Gulliver comes about
And bumps his rump into the steeple.

He hears the pastor's flaming shout:
"Things are not as important as people."
Seeing the giant Gulliver through the roof,
His congregation thinks pastor a bit aloof

So the good pastor says to the giant,
"I'll pull out your splinter, but dig me a well.
You still owe me for that steeple!"

Getting to the point, the giant replies:
"To hell with the well, this bee stings.
You said it yourself:
'People are more important than things.'"

Nextdoor is a social media app frequently used (and overused) for sharing neighborhood happenings and annoyances such as from dogs, alligators, traffic and people.

Heard on *Nextdoor*

Park Landing (PL): If you heard screaming just now, that was me and my two chihuahuas trying to get in my front door to avoid some vicious slithering animal. It came onto my porch snapping and growling. FINAL WARNING: I've posted this previously, and if it happens again, I'll defend myself.

Kay Todd Rd.: Don't shoot 'em, ma'm. Sounds like my pet alligator, 'cept he's generally friendlier. I moved here from Florida last fall, but he ran off shortly after, so I built a chicken coop. Thought he was gone, but sounds like he's taken a liking to Brunswick Forest.

Parkway Crossing: Wonder if he's the same gator I saw yesterday.

Park West: I think I saw him, too. Was he wearing sunglasses?

Parkway Crossing: Ya and walking upright.

Evangeline Place: Well, I can't say I saw him for sure, but a British chap rang my bell yesterday, and said he was thirsty. His breath smelled of fish, but I'm blind and widowed so I invited him in.

PL: Why?

Evangeline Place: Claimed he was cold-blooded but had a warm heart. He admitted he was new to the neighborhood, a bit lost and just needed to cool off.

Park West: That was nice of you. It was 98 degrees yesterday with 98% humidity.

Hazel Branch: That's BS. I caught him sleeping on my porch curled up like he owns the place. Almost didn't notice, he went so well with the décor. But no, he's a vagrant. I chased him with a rake.

Shelmore: So what did you do Evangeline?

Evangeline Place: I invited him in. Told him to sit in my easy chair and mixed a daquiri with a double shot of rum. He drank it in one gulp, then invited me to dance. He likes smooth jazz.

Park West: So is he handsome?

Evangeline Place: His hands are rough; definitely needs a manicure. Cyrano would envy his nose. He's definitely stylish though. He's got a thing for crocodile belts. And I'd say, a very good dancer. He didn't step on my feet anyway.

Park West: Sounds charming.

Evangeline Place: His accent reminds me of Peter O'Toole, but he calls himself 'Al.' Quite the conversationalist – and an environmentalist, too, like me. Al's very knowledgeable about wildlife, especially fish and birds, marshes, inland waterways, and stormwater runoff systems. But I managed to doze off when he got to microbiology. When I woke up, he was gone.

Hazel Branch: "OMG! Did he take anything? *...Check your silverware!*

Evangeline Place: No. In fact, he was very considerate: He trimmed my flowers; even emptied my kitchen garbage before he left. He did leave quite an odor in the bathroom though, but he did flush.

Hazel Branch: You sure nothing's gone?

Evangeline Place: Wait. I know I left a jar of wild herring in the fridge yesterday. --But I was sleeping. He was welcome to it.

PL: Well, he wasn't at all nice to me and my chihuahuas.

Kay Todd Rd.: You gotta admit, chihuahuas can be more annoying than a rooster at dawn. If you really want to make him go away, PL, just toss him a roaster (he loves Costco) or at least a cold leg.

Evangeline Place: And tell Al that Shirley at 1001 Evangeline would love to see him again, and if he brings flowers, I'll put on some cool jazz and open a jar of wild herring.

Jonah

I could have saved them if they had only listened. I mean somebody had to tell them, and I was the one who God appointed. Some would say "anointed," but I think "appointed" is the right word. I mean believe me, I didn't want to come to New York City, but this is where God told me to go. Still, I was what you'd call a reluctant customer.

The other crew members on the barge had already jettisoned all they could to lighten our load in the storm, but I told them that the seas would calm if they just threw me overboard. That's what God told me, and I was insistent about it. They were headed to Norfolk, but I said this is where I get off. The captain said I was so obnoxious he'd grant my wish.

So I was floundering, ready to drown in the choppy seas off Long Island, when I felt a tug on my feet. At first, I thought it was a shark, but no, it's the gums of a whale. Suddenly I'm sucked inside and travelling down his gullet. Now let me tell you, it was slimy, and the smell was overpowering. The darkness hugged me like a giant bag, and I was the garbage. But I could breathe.

I was getting mighty thirsty after the second day, but I was still breathing. My skin felt like I fell in vat of lemon juice, and it burned, which only sharpened by senses. I promised God that if He let me out, I would go to New York. Maybe I couldn't save the whole city, but maybe just one place.

The next morning, the whale burped me up like bad codfish. I washed ashore and after a long, hard nap it was almost dark. I walked and walked and came upon a beach with a bathhouse. Further up the boulevard, I found a laundromat. I explained to a young man folding his clothes that I had been shipwrecked and needed clothes. He looked at my tatters, then gave me these jeans and this NYU sweatshirt. I assured him God would bless him for his kindness. He then hands me a $20 and suggests I get something to eat.

When I saw "Bob's Burgers & Ale," I felt called to go in. The last thing I wanted was fish. So I ordered a burger with everything and a Bud on draft.

Now I know you're thinking, Jesus didn't drink, right? Oh, but he did. Remember, he turned water into wine, not grape soda. So I enjoyed my meal and then climbed atop the bar just like He told me to do. I did a jig with my beer in hand, then took a knife and clinked my glass to get everyone's attention.

I told them that I was a sinner and that God had sent me there to save them. When I told them that they worshipped idols, they jeered, but I reminded them that they all were chasing material things, and they all had a little toy of the devil in their hand that demanded too much of their attention.

I must've been pretty scary looking, and I thought they were getting it. One woman wondered why my skin was all mottled. I told them all I had been swallowed by a whale, and the stomach acid bleached me into a brown cow.

At this, one of the guys playing pool, tells me to get down off the bar. When I responded with another jig, he took the cue stick and swiped it at my legs. I fell right on top of him. Now it wasn't my fault that he hit the corner of a table and was now bleeding on the floor. They all looked at me.

What was I to do? I grabbed the other cue stick and started swinging it to keep him and the others away. Then I backed toward the door and ran.

The police picked me up about a block away and brought me to you. Now I bet you don't believe me either, but they said you would listen. Maybe I didn't need to save the city, or the folks at Bob's Burger & Ale. Maybe it was just you.

Author's Note:

As a skeptical sort, I often wondered why the people of Nineveh would ever have believed the washed-up Jonah. I mean, could anyone survive inside a whale, let alone for three days? While I was mulling this over in the mid-'90s, I happened across a blurb in the *The New York Times.* A sailor from the Middle East was rescued by a naval ship after spending three days in the ocean – inside a whale! For anyone who thought "Jonah" might be a fish tale, our Middle Eastern sailor had olive skin, but after his ordeal *his entire body was mottled with white splotches.*

God Is with Me I Declare

God is with me I declare
He does conquer all despair.

Into the darkness I cannot see
But His loving presence surrounds me.
Not the touch of a petal I feel
I yearn for a voice, a bell to peal.

A stronger heart might sense it out
Yet even Moses wrestled with doubt.

Faith must fly above without a net
Face all torrents, all that is yet.

Sacred Heart breathes in the souls of men
But each man must breathe it out again.

Author's Note:
I wrote this in early 2011, a time of uncertainty for many still climbing out of the Great Recession. A few months later, God set me on higher ground -- and He has blessed me in many ways since.

Shrouded in Mystery

"Gentlemen, we have to work quickly. The caretaker of the Cathedral starts his rounds at 6 a.m."

It was now approaching midnight and they were an hour away. "I hear you, Padre. I'm working as fast as I can." Martino Rusconi, PhD, a world-renowned archeologist and expert in ancient linens, adjusted his headlamp. He did not appreciate being rushed, and under the circumstances felt comfortable calling the Archbishop of Torino, 'padre.' After all, it was the great Archbishop Fernando V. Dotellini who had come to him. Even if it irritated the 'padre,' the familiarity made Martino comfortable, and it was his steady hands that counted.

Dr. Rusconi shut out the sound of the laboratory's twin mega-volt generators as they started to whir. Gently he worked tiny hooks and a tweezer to loosen and pull at a single, horizontal thread below the facial image on the flaxen cloth. The herringbone weave was consistent with burial cloths of noblemen in the 1st Century -- and one of the main reasons he went 'all in' on this surreptitious expedition. The sum the church would pay for his expertise was paltry compared to the magnitude of the discovery -- and who else would the world believe?

After two hours, Dr. Rusconi extracted a 30 cm (1 ft.) length of flax without damage to the rest of the shroud. His fibrous sample broke in several places during the process, but that did not matter now. A third of the material was prepared and placed in a pyrolytic chamber; the remainder saved for further testing and verification.

The accelerated mass spectrometer (AMS) was operated by Dr. Francois Bertrand who earned a PhD in physics from the Sorbonne and owned the physics lab on the outskirts of Milano. A devout Catholic, Francois had been an only child. When his parents took him to the Shrine of Mary at Lourdes at age nine, he felt a presence, a spiritual awakening, that deeply affected him. He never found science and faith incompatible, and in fact, he believed one could bolster the other. At 37, he was now a leader in the international physics community, and well known for his generous heart and honesty.

Dr. Rusconi recognized that Dr. Bertrand and his state-of-the-art test laboratory were playing a vital role. Yet while the method of carbon dating was accurate and straightforward, sampling was critical. In 1988, when the shroud was first tested using mass spectrometry, the sample required for testing was by comparison, large. It came from a rectangular corner of the shroud which, it was later discovered, was likely repaired by nuns in medieval times following one of the shroud's many moves. So the three independent labs produced similar date ranges. They were in all probability correct in dating the cloth between 1260 and 1390 CE -- but it was all wrong. A sample from the central portion of the shroud was needed, however, the Catholic church had steadfastly refused further testing after the firestorm.

A sample only a fraction of the size was needed now. It seemed to take an eternity for the generators to charge and the two-tiered accelerators to cycle up to speed, but soon the trio would have their answer. The three men watched through a small window of the heating chamber as the fragments burst into light and disappeared with a puff. The ash was sucked away, stripped of lower isotopes to form pure graphite, and then inserted into the accelerator for bombardment by high energy ions so the spectrometer could measure the total C14.

The archbishop and archeologist watched over Dr. Bertrand's shoulder as a pronounced spike appeared on his screen. The physicist captured what he needed on a flash drive and sealed it in a plastic envelope. The archbishop was anxious: "So, *when*, when is it?"

"I can date it between 20 BCE and 50 CE, with a 95% confidence level."

A silence filled the lab as if a cotton cloud from heaven had fallen from the sky and pushed out all the air. In his heart, Archbishop Dotellini had felt certain they would achieve this result, but now confronted with the reality, he felt dumbfounded and amazed. A puff of air exited his lungs in relief. He'd taken a huge risk in removing the shroud and conducting this test on his own authority. His longtime friend, Monsignor Michael Givino, rector of the Cathedral of St. John the Baptist in Torino, had convinced him that the shroud was more than an icon of the Catholic Church. It was a sacred relic that needed to be elevated to its proper place in human history. A definitive finding would attract new members and help restore the reputation of the church after so many scandals, including a number in the archdiocese.

The scandals the archbishop knew only too well after 28 years in the church. A ray of sun now pierced the high windows of the laboratory and broke his trance: "The three of us must report this in person to the Holy See at once."

"We must replace the shroud at once, or we'll be arrested," Dr. Rusconi said. "I'm going to write this up with Dr. Bertrand so Rome can read it in *Mass Spectrometry* like everyone else. --Now give me a hand, gentleman."

In the hour drive back to Torino in the laboratory's van, the archbishop agreed that the pair should report their findings as soon as possible -- and they would benefit greatly from the Vatican's help. The Vatican would give them access to the church's archives and assist them, adding depth and credibility to their findings. Dr. Bertrand found this spiritually, if not scientifically, compelling, and assisted in persuading the reluctant physicist.

Dr. Rusconi was less interested in metaphysics as the historic authenticity of the shroud, and the inevitable notoriety. But he knew he couldn't do the science justice without Dr. Bertrand who would like to do right by the church. But the Catholic Church? Well, the Vatican would slow the process. Still, the archbishop and Dr. Bertrand persisted and convinced him that it was wise to acquaint himself with those in the church hierarchy who could bolster their claim.

When Dr. Rusconi finally agreed, Dr. Bertrand smiled. "Just think, Martino, with the Pope's blessing on our work, perhaps the Holy Spirit will finally penetrate that lump of graphite you call a heart."

The back door of the Cathedral was opened by Monsignor Givino at 5:28 a.m. The rector helped replace the shroud in its heavy black frame on the floor, then the men hoisted it up using pulleys suspended from hooks on the ceiling. They carefully secured it to the wall just minutes before the caretaker arrived. The shroud had been away from the Cathedral less than 12 hours.

Archbishop Dotellini and Dr. Bertrand jumped into Dr. Rusconi's van at 5:57 a.m. and headed for Rome, about an 8-hour drive. At 7 a.m., the archbishop would contact Cardinal Giamatti Rosetti at the Vatican, an archeologist trained church historian, and the papal city's resident expert on the Shroud of Turin. With his agreement, Cardinal Rosetti would request an urgent audience with the Holy Father.

Cardinal Rosetti fumed when he heard. "You not only tampered with one of the church's most important treasures, you physically damaged it. I should have been informed. The Holy Father should have been informed. And now you want my help?"

Archbishop Dotellini let the cardinal vent until the steam ran out. The two men had known each other for more than 25 years and generally understood one another. The archbishop explained that he did not want to put the cardinal in jeopardy by involving him before they knew the answer. Then he agreed with the cardinal: "Yes, we tampered with one of the church's most important treasures, but that is now *finito, perfectus, fait accompli,* and I am coming to you now. It is time for the church to move forward. The way to do that is with new scientific and historical facts, which we now have. It is time for the church to step out of the darkness, to enlighten the world with the light of the universe. I know you understand, cardinal, that the time for this revelation is at hand. It could not have happened before. We needed only a thread, and this Pope is the one for such a time as this."

He knew the Cardinal would understand the nuanced reference to the time. In the Book of Esther, the Jewish princess risks her life at a critical moment to influence her husband, the King of Persia, to save the Jewish people who were living in bondage. An evil man named Haman had inveigled the King to sign an edict suggesting an organized mass slaughter. When the King learned his wife was a Jewess, he might have killed her on the spot. However, because of his love for Esther, he reviewed his records and discovered a way to rescue the Jewish people from his own incontrovertible edict.

After some resistance, Cardinal Rosetti acquiesced. He agreed to contact the Holy Father's personal secretary to arrange a short meeting at the Pope's earliest convenience. The Cardinal was not at all certain how the Pope would react, and so while he would attend, he did not want to be the messenger. When he contacted the Pope's secretary, the cardinal emphasized that he did not know the exact details. "However, it concerns a vital matter of church history that could be of global importance, and they request an urgent audience with the Holy Father sometime after 2:30 p.m. today."

The cardinal was aware that the Pope had a grueling daily schedule and might miss his afternoon nap, but that the secretary, in all likelihood, could make it happen. Twenty minutes later, the meeting was set for 3:30 p.m. The Cardinal mused to himself, "So maybe the Pope would get his nap after all."

Cardinal Rosetti conveyed the news to the three at 10 a.m. but begged off a late lunch to avoid anyone drawing unwarranted conclusions. He already knew all he needed to know. It was spectacular information, but what happened next would depend entirely on the Pope's response.

At 3:25 p.m. the Cardinal met the trio outside the Pope's study, and at 3:30 p.m. the secretary ushered them all in. Archbishop Dotellini made the introductions and was the first to kiss the Pope's ring. Drs. Bertrand and Rusconi then followed his lead, and the three sat in armchairs in front of the Pope's ornate desk. Next, Cardinal Rosetti smiled and leaned in to kiss the ring. "Greetings, Holy Father. Good to see you again." He thought the Pope seemed perturbed, perhaps from lack of sleep. He took his place on the wine-colored settee and tried to relax.

The Pope bowed his head and asked the Lord for wisdom and guidance in all things. Then he looked up brightly at each of the three men. "So I understand you have some news for me. Judging from who you are and the little bit I have been told so far, I surmise that this momentous news concerns the shroud of Turin."

Archbishop Dotellini spoke first: "Indeed, it is true, Holy Father. We have new evidence that proves with a high degree of certainty that the shroud is from the time of our Lord and Savior."

"Can you be more specific?"

The archbishop glanced at the physicist.

"We have dated the cloth to between 20 BC and 50 AD, a 70-year span, with a 95% confidence level." Rusconi was careful to use the church's Anno Domini dating reference to avoid irritation.

"And you believe this is a replicable result?"

"Yes, there may be some variations depending on the specifics of the laboratory equipment and test protocols. But as I'm sure you are aware from the 1988 carbon dating, the range from the three laboratories varied but was all within 90 years."

The Pope smiled again, his eyes twinkling. "And only off by 12 Centuries."

Rusconi couldn't help but chortle. Archbishop Dotellini and Dr. Bertrand smiled along; the cardinal just nodded sideways.

"That's right, Your Holiness, all because of where the sample came from."

"And where did yours come from?"

"It was Dr. Bertrand's turn to answer. "A single, 30 cm thread from the center of the cloth, about a third of the way from the top."

The Pope rubbed his chin, musing. "I see. So this thread too came from the Shroud of Torino."

"Of course, only from the original linen in which the body was wrapped, not a 13th Century patch."

"And who authorized this sample?" The Pope snapped his head toward the settee. "Did you know about this Cardinal Rosetti?"

"I first heard about it only this morning, Your Holiness, and I am learning these new facts, just as you."

"I authorized it, Your Holiness." The Archbishop's voice was more strident than apologetic. "It was my decision. There are many in my archdiocese and beyond who understand the church suffered a serious blow from the original findings, and another by its failure to aggressively pursue the truth."

The Pope was not smiling anymore. "Is that all?"

Archbishop Dotellini continued. "We must also consider the larger context, Your Holiness. The truth of wayward priests, consumed by lust, driven to unspeakable acts has harmed many thousands -- more than we can know. The coverups compounded that pain, and only intensified the Church's bleeding both in members and in spirit. There is resignation rather than renewal, heartache rather than hope in our mother church."

The Pope looked away, seemingly studying the shelves of ecclesiastical books surrounding them. Then he locked eyes with the archbishop. "Do you think, archbishop, that I am unaware, that I do not see or feel this pain, this weltschmerz that pervades our Church -- the subterranean sadness of our laity and clerics who want nothing more than God's glory to shine through all the good that the Church does in the world for the health and well-being of our fellow man?"

The archbishop's first reaction was to protest. Of course he knew that the scandals occupied the Pope's thoughts and prayers, and that the Church, under the Pope's leadership, was accepting some blame and working to support investigations and compensate accusers who pursued their claims in court.

Certainly, the Pope was also aware that the scandals had created a black hole threatening church finances. Declining attendance and the mass exodus, including many wealthy donors, had meant a massive divestiture of church properties around the world, even if not in Italy where 96% of the population was baptized Catholic. Yes, he knew the Pope knew all these things, but a sudden embarrassment overtook him. Under his cassock, sweat poured profusely, trickling from armpits and down his back. He kept silent.

The Pope's face was now pink, his jaw set. "Did you think you had the authority to conduct this investigation because you knew better? It is I who am the vicar of Christ, not you, Archbishop *Dotellini.*" He spit out the name. "What you have done is sinful and has violated the very vestments you wear."

The archbishop dipped his head. "And for this I must ask your forgiveness, for I have sinned not only against God, but against you."

The Pope did not immediately respond, and it was Dr. Bertrand's turn to risk an interjection and soften the apostolic sting. "I assure you, Holy Father, I too am a sinner in this, equally, if not more so, than the archbishop, for it was my hand that extracted the sample. So I too must plead for mercy and beg your forgiveness. For you, too, Holy Father, are keenly aware of the spiritual significance of our actions. However grievous, I know in my heart *all things work together for good to them that love God, to them who are called according to his purpose.* And I know you too believe this, for you asked us a question about replicability of this test at the outset that is burning on all our hearts. With your permission, I would like to answer."

"Proceed, my son."

"Yes, it's replicable. When I extracted this one single thread, it was enough for two more tests." Dr. Bertrand turned his head to Dr. Rusconi.

"I'm the other sinner here, Father. I'm the one…"

The archbishop instantly corrected Rusconi. "You mean, Your Holiness."

The Pope seemed more relaxed now. "It's OK, continue."

"Your Holiness, I'm the one who performed this test using state-of-the-art accelerated mass spectroscopy, AMS for short. It's far more sensitive than the mass spec used in 1988, and only a few hundred milligrams of material are needed to duplicate the test.

"We can share the remaining fragments with whatever laboratories you choose. If they use essentially the same AMS equipment and follow precisely the same test protocol as my lab in Milano, we can expect the carbon dating ranges to be similar, though they may vary by some years on either end.

"You say, 'you can expect them to be similar within some range… Is there a chance that they will not?"

Dr. Rusconi explained that if tests are performed without error on the same strand, the chance of an aberrant result would be near zero. The remainder of the sample was locked in a temperature- and humidity-controlled cabinet in Milano.

"Near zero. So what do you believe is the chance that the man etched on the shroud is our Lord and Savior?"

"My belief does not matter. That, Your Holiness, is a question for Dr. Bertrand."

"Why do you think your belief does not matter, my son? I assure you that from where I sit, it very much does."

"Well, it either is or it isn't, but AMS testing cannot determine that."

Dr. Bertrand felt compelled to explain two other key facts which, taken together, would lead most logical minds to a singular conclusion. First, the herringbone pattern, consistent with the time of Christ's crucifixion circa 33 AD; why would a criminal of Rome be buried in a cloth of this quality? According to the Bible, Joseph of Arimathea, a wealthy man and disciple, asked Pontius Pilate for the body and buried Jesus in a tomb he had hewn into a rock.

Second was the image itself. Dr. Bertrand produced his tablet computer and placed it on the Pope's desk. The full-length image showed the crucified body of a man in a faint sepia tone on the 14 ft. linen, hands folded below his waist. Then he switched to the photographic negative revealing details in startling *bas relief*. The man, about 5 ft. 7 inches tall, bears the marks of Roman crucifixion including wounds consistent with a crown of thorns. The image is human blood, confirmed by DNA to be from a male, type AB. Further DNA testing also confirmed some of the pollen present on the cloth to be from the Middle East.

"But how did the image get there? How did the blood of this man become etched in the cloth?" Dr. Bertrand answered his own question.

"You already know the answer, Holy Father, but to me this is the capstone: Radiation as powerful as the sun projected the image to the inner side of the cloth. This alone is astounding and is confirmed by optical analysis. But the image is not just on one side, but front and back. So it wasn't like the body was simply left out in the sun. What's more, the blood isn't confined to the inner layer of the cloth. It is also registered in the topmost fibers of the linen with minimal distortion. This transfer can be explained by chemical action, specifically a water-or-oil based solution catalyzed by the presence of aloes and myrrh."

"Those were expensive emollients and fragrances used to dress the body of a nobleman," Rusconi commented not wanting to appear uninformed.

"Yes," Bertrand continued. "So the image transfer was like a snapshot, a sudden exposure of light altering the chemical emulsion on the surface of film. The face appears clear, but you can see that blood flowed from the gash in the lower abdomen and streamed behind the man's hands to his loins."

The Roman soldiers conducting a crucifixion in 1st Century Jerusalem worked from early morning into midday as the criminal carried the cross through jeering crowds in the streets and up Golgotha hill which overlooked the city. Normally, the bodies would hang for days. In the case of Christ's crucifixion, because it was just before Sabbath preceding the Passover feast, the Jewish high priests asked Pilate for the soldiers to break the legs of the condemned to hasten death so the bodies could be buried before sunset, as prescribed in Deuteronomy 21:22–23.

On the lower part of the cross, there was an angled block which the criminal would need to press against to stretch upright and breathe. This made each breath excruciating. Breaking the legs would intensify the pain and the prisoner would quickly suffocate. However, in the case of Jesus, it appeared he was already dead so there was no need to break his legs. The soldier pierced his abdomen to make sure.

The archbishop muttered, "And not a bone was broken." If no bones were broken, it fulfilled three biblical prophecies. Exodus 12:43,46 *And the Lord said to Moses and Aaron, "This is the ordinance of the Passover…, nor shall you break one of its bones."* Numbers 9:12 *They shall leave none of it until morning, nor break one of its bones. According to all the ordinances of the Passover they shall keep it.* In both these verses, 'it' refers to the sacrificial lamb of Passover. And Psalms 34:20 *"He guards all his bones; not one of them is broken."* 'His' refers to a righteous man of God.

The Pope nodded slowly and thanked Dr. Bertrand. He then turned his attention back to Dr. Rusconi. "Does this increase your faith?"

It was Dr. Rusconi who was discomfited now. He shifted in his chair, and there was a yawing pause before he answered. "Well, yes, Your Holiness, even though my mother is Scandinavian my father is Italian, so growing up I was steeped in Church dogma."

"But do you believe it?"

"I am a man of science, so I believe whatever the facts tell me. The new carbon dating combined with Dr. Bertrand's analysis does in all probability confirm that the shroud is a 1st Century burial cloth of a man who died by crucifixion, if not definitively the burial cross of Christ. Many will agree. But still others will dispute our claims by attacking our methods and try to poke holes in our arguments, particularly the metaphysical ones."

The Pope nodded as if he understood Rusconi clearly now. "So you believe in science, including the new fact that you brought here today, and the explanation of how this image was formed, but you do not believe that this is enough to prove that this man was the Messiah, the Paschal lamb?"

"As I said, my opinion does not matter, and I must remain objective to maintain my credibility and that of the scientific evidence."

"I do appreciate your candidness, Dr. Rusconi. Because of that I want to share something with all of you that I received three days ago by private messenger from Monsignor Givino, the rector of the Cathedral of St. John the Baptist, who you may know."

The Pope pulled a key from his robe and unlocked the bottom drawer of his desk, producing a large manila envelope. "When I received this, I immediately contacted the rector and swore him to secrecy. I have been praying for guidance and wrestling in my heart what to do, so I have shared this with no one."

The Pope handed the envelope to Dr. Rusconi and then turned toward the Cardinal. "When you contacted my office this morning, the coincidence startled me, but I know God often speaks this way."

Several minutes passed as the physicist skimmed the abstract and flipped through the images as the others watched. When he appeared to have finished, the cardinal leaned forward on the settee and was the first to speak: "So, Dr. Rusconi, pray tell."

"Apparently, ours was not the first scientific test Monsignor Givino arranged. A scientist from the Italian National Research Council took a millimeter-sized sample about a month ago. He evaluated it using a new method called Wide-angle X-ray Scattering, or WAXS for short. It's not as accurate as radiocarbon dating, but it corroborates our finding, and dates the linen to the 1st Century."

The assembled crowd let out a whoop at the news as the Pope observed the spirited reaction. The archbishop couldn't help but wonder why the Pope had been so harsh on him. Perhaps the previous experiment had also taken him by surprise. Would he admonish Monsignor Givino again or be gratified by the new findings? "So you have clarity now, Your Holiness?"

The Pope tilted his head. He was gazing at Dr. Rusconi. "Does this increase your faith, my son."

"It is another important piece of the puzzle and makes me almost certain that more testing will reinforce these results."

"I had hoped for an answer from the Lord, and now, thanks to you Dr. Rusconi, I have it." He looked around the room at each of them. "There should be no more testing."

Everyone was incredulous. The blood rushed from Dr. Rusconi's face. The archbishop protested: "But Holy Father, I don't understand…"

"Don't you see? As believers, we already have all the evidence we need. We now have scientific corroboration on the dating, bolstering our belief that this is the burial cloth of Messiah. But even if our skeptics believe this new evidence, will we have proven that he also rose from the dead?"

"But the cloth, the radiation and the registration of the image, all point to that conclusion," said Dr. Bertrand.

"Yes, and as the Apostle Paul tells us in Hebrews 11: *Faith is the substance of things hoped for, the evidence of things not seen.* Yet for skeptics there is never enough proof. They may not be able to genuinely experience what is right in front of them because their hearts won't allow it."

"What do you mean?" Dr. Rusconi blurted.

"It is just as in the day when Jesus raised Lazarus from the dead. When he asked for the stone to be rolled away, his family wasn't sure they wanted this miracle. They were concerned about the stench since Lazarus had been dead for four days. Of course, Jesus calls his friend to come out for the benefit of all assembled there. Lazarus inches forward, and his friends unwrap the cloth. His skin has not decayed. He's all right. Everyone is astonished; but not all are happy.

"Some believe, but some go to the Pharisees. They wonder: 'If Jesus was really Lazarus' friend, why did he not rescue him before he died?' They are eyewitnesses to a resurrection, but they cannot see the power and goodness of the man who made this miracle happen. The Pharisees, feeling their power threatened, plot to kill Jesus to save the nation."

Dr. Rusconi did his best to calm himself before he asked: "So how does that change anything?"

"Yes, how? That is exactly my point. If you publish your results, with or without further replication, I now understand clearly that it won't change anything in the minds of skeptics, or…"

Dr. Rusconi felt the Pope's eyes boring through him and did not need the Pope to finish his sentence.

Archbishop Dotellini felt the energy of their mission slipping away: "What of believers, your Holiness, and the reputation of the church?"

"Yes, you make a good point, archbishop. And I suppose Dr. Rusconi, as a scientist, you will publish your research in any case, just as I suspect our other Italian scientists will, regardless of what I say. However, the church cannot appear to influence the research in any way, so we will step back."

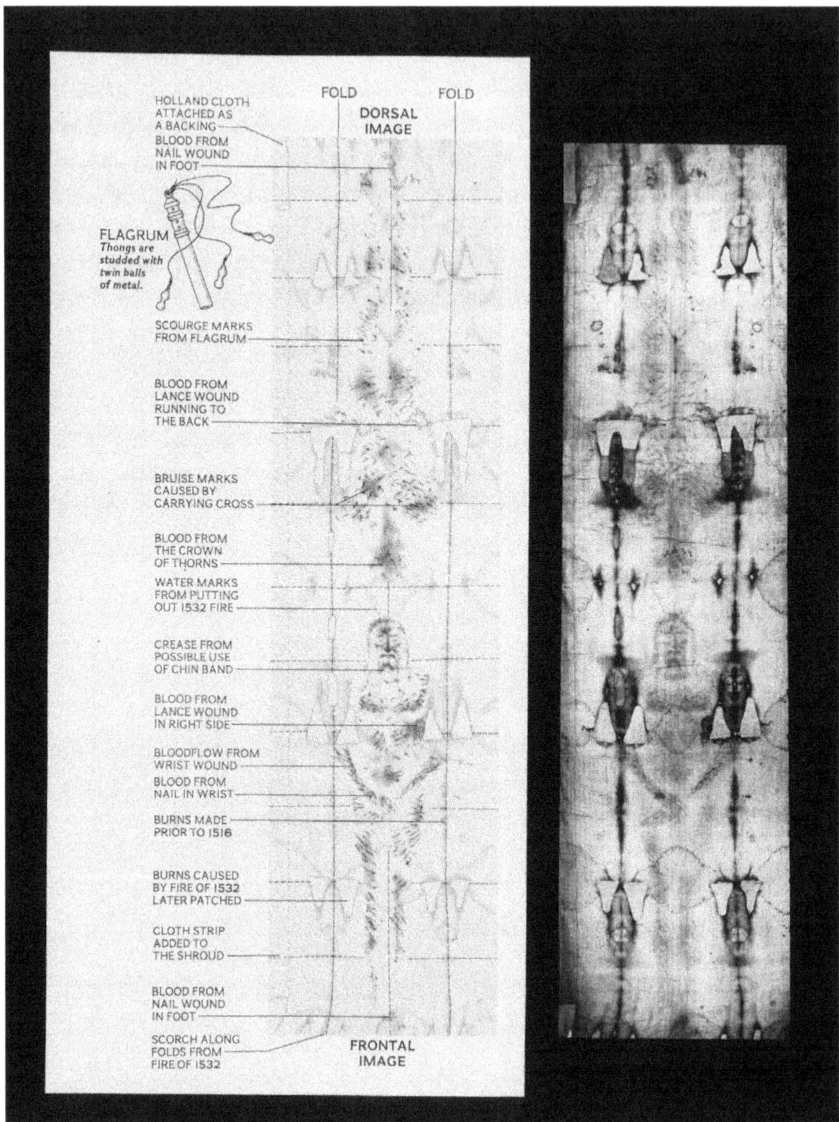

A full body image of the shroud and notations from the
Shroud of Turin collection of scientific photographer
Vernon Miller. To view this (image 037[7]) in color from
this 1978 collection visit www.shroudphotos.com

The Pope rose from his chair and the meeting was over. The Cardinal was as disappointed as any of them and did supply helpful materials backchannel to Dr. Bertrand. Drs. Rusconi and Bertrand did publish their paper after sending the remaining samples to two other labs for independent testing. The three labs coordinated publication in peer-reviewed journals in the same month for maximum impact.

The new research, including the X-ray scattering testing, gained international news coverage in 2022. Some of it can still be found on the Internet for anyone who would search. Yet there has been no swell in church attendance, no mass pilgrimages to Torino or the Holy Land, and the problems of the world seem more intense than ever. Believers though understand that "the leaf is on the fig tree," and Messiah will be appearing soon.

Author's Note:
Except for the fictional account of the new Accelerated Mass Spectrometry (AMS) testing, the science in this story is true, and the background on the shroud is based on the historical record. This fictional story started as a 20-minute writing exercise in March 2023. I felt compelled to expound on the first 400 words and finish the story as Easter approached--yet I didn't know exactly how it would end. As I was drafting the scene at the Vatican, I happened to check another detail about the shroud, and to my surprise discovered the 2022 tests using Wide-Array X-ray Scattering (WAXS). While WAXS is not as accurate as carbon dating with AMS, it does support the theory that the shroud is the burial cloth of Jesus Christ.